*Additional* ~~*praise for*~~

# IN THE EVEN'

"Spare, haunting, and mesmerizing, ~~the stories~~ ~~in~~ ~~In~~ tact somehow capture the ungraspable essence of being human. This book, these characters, put a spell on me."

—Diane Cook, author of the Booker finalist *The New Wilderness*

"Rohan's book of short stories examines something similar to [the horror of our pandemic isolation] in its evocation of what connection or its lack can do to us. *In the Event of Contact* is a loving homage to humanity in all its complexity."

— *The Millions*

"These characters long for connections that keep eluding them: they feel so much and yet can touch so little. Their tragedies and resilience are brilliantly various and individual—none alike, and none exactly like ours—but they speak to the universal through the particular as only art can manage. A tremendous achievement."

—Clare Beams, author of *The Illness Lesson*

"Beautiful, startling, disarming, and honest, *In the Event of Contact* is disquieting and compelling in equal measure."

—Danielle McLaughlin, author of *The Art of Falling*

"Each of these stories is beautifully-written, wise and wry; read as a collection, their cumulative effect is gently devastating. With the lightest hand, Rohan has delivered a meditation on what it is to be human: surrounded by people, quite alone and perpetually craving connection."

—Louise Kennedy, author of
*The End of the World is a Cul De Sac*

"Rohan's plain prose helps to feature the emotional earthquakes these characters undergo while they're navigating ordinary happenings, and her masterful use of Irish lilts and rhythms helps to reveal intricate emotional distances between those who left and those who stayed behind."

—*Foreword Reviews*

# IN THE EVENT OF CONTACT

## ALSO BY ETHEL ROHAN

*Cut Through the Bone*
*Goodnight Nobody*
*The Weight of Him*

# IN THE EVENT
# OF CONTACT

## STORIES

ETHEL ROHAN

**DZANC
BOOKS**

5220 Dexter Ann Arbor Rd.
Ann Arbor, MI 48103
www.dzancbooks.org

Library of Congress Cataloguing-in-Publication Data available upon request.

ISBN: 9781950539260
First US edition: May 2021
Interior design by Michelle Dotter

Grateful acknowledgement is made to the editors of the publications in which the following stories first appeared:

"Everywhere She Went," *The Irish Times*
"UNWANTED," *The Lonely Crowd*
"Collisions," winner of the Bryan MacMahon Short Story Award. Judge, Eilís Ní Dhuibhne. *Listowel Writers' Week Winners' Anthology.*
"At the Side of the Road," *BANSHEE Literary Magazine*
"Before Storms Had Names," *BULL Magazine*
"The Great Blue Open," *The Irish Times*

Printed in the United States of America

10   9   8   7   6   5   4   3   2   1

*for Survivors.*

# CONTENTS

"My life burned inside me. Even such as it was, it was the only record of me, and it was my only creation, and something in me would not accept that it was insignificant."

—Nuala O'Faolain, author of *Are You Somebody?*

# IN THE EVENT OF CONTACT

RUTH, MARY, AND I were identical triplets. I was the oldest by ten minutes, Mary was in the middle, and Ruth, the youngest, was infamous. Ruth's saga started in kindergarten and ever after people remained divided over whether she was a weirdo, the victim of a genuine disorder, or plain bad.

The bother began with our five-year-old classmate, Timmy White. At every opportunity, Timmy insisted on tracing his fingertips over any flash of Ruth's bare skin. The afternoon he dipped his fingers into the hollow of Ruth's throat, she suffered a seizure.

After, Ruth claimed she couldn't stand to be touched, not by anyone, not ever. Doctors confirmed the crippling fear was a real and rare phobia. I could never understand, though, why Ruth's no-contact rule extended to Mary and me, the two people closest to her in the whole world.

We were twelve years old, and nearing the end of primary school, when Ruth's phobia deteriorated to an especially disturbing degree. If anyone accidentally touched her, even the barest brush, she screamed and dropped to the ground in a fit. The neighborhood kids and our fellow students grew ever more frightened and repelled by her, and no one wanted to be around her.

"How's she ever going to get on in life?" Dad said.

"The school should have done more to stop that boy back then," Mam said.

I seemed to be the only one angry with Ruth. She needed to get over her bizarre fear and return to herself, to us. Let our family get back to normal.

"Why do you always have to go on about it? She can't help it," Mary said.

Toward the end of summer and the start of secondary school, our family's panic was at an all-time high, worrying how Ruth could possibly attend classes with her now utter intolerance. Only I wasn't convinced Ruth's phobia was as crippling as she claimed. During a family day out at Dollymount Strand, I watched her brave the sand, pebbles, shells, seaweed, and salty ocean. How could she withstand all those irritants? At home later, Jimmy, our cockatoo, perched on her hand, shoulders, and head. If his antics didn't offend her either, why couldn't Mary and I, her two-thirds, also touch her?

As soon as I got Ruth alone, I quizzed her. She fired her sandy shoe at me, sending granules flying. "It's *people* touching me I can't stand. It's like slugs slithering over my skin, covering me in slime. It's bad enough that other people don't believe me, but for you to accuse me—"

"I just want you to get better." I watched her cry, aching to hug her and envying the tears sliding down her red-splotched face, able to make tender contact.

✺

The start of secondary school loomed. I tried to convince Mary we were the only ones who could fix Ruth.

"I don't know," she said nervously.

"Listen to me. We need to trick her into recovery. Otherwise, she's going to be shunned and miserable at school, and us along with her."

"What if we hurt her?"

"We can't. We're a part of her. If she can touch herself, then we can touch her, too. Once she realizes that, that's the beginning of the end of all this."

I entered our parents' empty bedroom and pulled open the bottom drawer in the tall rosewood cabinet opposite their bed, where Mam housed our few keepsakes. I sneaked two of the three pairs of long white gloves from the drawer and placed them under my pillow. The gloves, soft, silky, and blessed during our First Holy Communion mass, were ideal.

Mary and I waited until late that night, when Ruth had fallen asleep. At my whispered instruction we climbed out of our bunk beds, pulled on the gloves, and tiptoed across the wiry carpet to Ruth's single bed. We stood over her, my eyes adjusting to the dark, my nerves refusing to steady. I nodded at Mary. But she shook her head and took a step backward. When she couldn't be persuaded, I reached out a shaky hand and touched Ruth's face with my polyester fingertip, the gentlest flutter along her cheekbone. Ruth shot up, screaming and thrashing.

Mam and Dad came running. After Mam calmed Ruth down, she worked the story out of Mary. Mam pulled the gloves off Mary's hands, and tugged them even more roughly from mine. She raised her arm and slapped the gloves across my face. Mary's hand rushed to her mouth. Ruth remained sitting on her bed, her knees hugged to her chest. Dad looked away.

⁓⦿⦾⦿⁓

Despite every possible precaution, Ruth lasted three days in secondary school. A fellow first-year student either forgot or ignored the warnings and touched Ruth's bare forearm. Ruth collapsed onto the schoolyard, hitting her head. She started convulsing, only the whites of her eyes showing. Blood filled the crack between her lips.

After Ruth recovered from her bit tongue and concussion, our parents brought her to see yet more doctors. Each agreed that Ruth was high-need and high-risk and required specialized schooling and care, at least until she showed signs of improvement. Our parents argued like never before.

"She wants more attention from you, they all do," Dad said.

"She got this from your side. You're a bunch of oddballs," Mam said. Dad's face slackened and dimmed, as if she'd also hit him across the cheek with something holy and stinging.

In addition to her office job, Mam started waitressing three nights a week in Flanagan's Restaurant in town. Dad, a life insurance agent by day, also found night work as a security guard at Smurfit printworks in Glasnevin. All so they could afford a private teacher for Ruth. One of Mam's longtime bosses recommended Mr. Doherty, a family friend and a tutor trained in special needs. After a phone interview, Mam invited Mr. Doherty to meet with us.

Right at three o'clock on Sunday afternoon, the doorbell rang. Jimmy stirred in his cage and flapped his white wings, showing their yellow underside. "Toodaloo." Mam answered the door and led Mr. Doherty into the living room. He shook each of our hands in turn, his palm sweaty. His gray eyes seemed too loose in his head and too much blood pooled in their inner corners, making me squeamish. When he reached Ruth, he pressed his hand to the breast of his leather jacket and delivered a tiny bow. "Nice to meet you." He dropped his arm to his side, its oily handprint leaving a shadow over his heart.

"What do we have here?" he said, moving to inspect Jimmy.

After a quick chat among the adults about cockatoos, we sat down, five of us surrounding the coffee table cluttered with china, tea, fancy biscuits, and triangular sandwiches topped with sprigs of parsley. Dad was left with nowhere to sit and remained standing in front of the empty fireplace.

From Dad's armchair, Mr. Doherty appraised Ruth, Mary, and me, sitting opposite him on the couch. We were long and thin, with brown eyes, browner bobs, straight lips, and milky skin with blue trails. "Remarkable," he said.

"Carbon copies," Mam said, pleased with herself.

"Yet each unique," he said.

I started to almost like him.

Mary pressed her hands together prayer-like and held them out. "See, my right pinkie is longer than my left. Theirs are the same size." She sounded triumphant.

Mr. Doherty crossed the room and pinched the tip of her extra long pinkie. "Isn't that something?"

She grinned, her lips glued back.

"That's enough, Triplet," Mam said, her voice as harsh as her smoker's cough.

Mary placed her hands beneath her thighs and seemed to fold in on herself, like air leaking from a blow-up doll.

Mr. Doherty returned to Dad's armchair. Mam perched on her chair next to him, her face speckled with gold bronzer. Mr. Doherty helped himself to a second sugar cookie. As he spoke, listing off his years of experience, he spat golden crumbs. His shirt collar cut into his neck and reddened skin bubbled over its white ridge. I kept expecting his top button to pop and fire into the air.

"This is going to work beautifully, don't you think, Ruth?" Mam said.

Ruth nodded, smiling. Mr. Doherty winked. She crossed her legs, her smile widening. Mr. Doherty eyed her bare knee, a tiny bald head.

Mam walked Mr. Doherty to the front door, Dad and the rest of us trailing.

Jimmy sang out. "Toodaloo."

Mam laughed. "You'll get used to him. He does that every time someone comes or goes."

"What an interesting household you have," Mr. Doherty said, holding Mam's hand with both of his. Her eyes sparkled brighter than her face bronzer.

⟁

The next day, Mary and I arrived home from school to find Mr. Doherty and Ruth tucked inside the back kitchen, the now study space. They sat at the white wooden table from the charity shop, their bodies as close as they could get without touching. Mam entered the main kitchen, her face opening with surprise when she saw Mary and me. Yet she was the one out of place, not usually home from the office until sixish. "How was school?" she said. Before we could answer, she smiled at Mr. Doherty. "Not as good as Ruth's first day, I bet."

She removed her navy cardigan and readied a pot of tea, her ivory blouse bringing out her creamy complexion. Mary and I set on two bowls of crunchy cornflakes. Mam carried a steaming cup and saucer into the study, our rose-patterned china out again for Mr. Doherty. He accepted the offering, his eyes gleaming. My stomach fluttered worse than when I was in an elevator, falling through a building.

Mam returned to the kitchen and cracked open a can of white lemonade, unleashing a hiss. "Can I tempt you to stay for dinner, Mr. Doherty? I'll make my chicken curry." She raised her heavily penciled eyebrows. "Unless you don't like spicy?"

"Oh I do," Mr. Doherty said.

"What time will Dad be home?" I said.

Ruth scratched her neck and tugged the vee of her blouse, complaining she felt hot and itchy. "It's like my clothes were washed in acid."

"Put your lotion on," Mam said.

"I already did," Ruth said, sounding tortured.

A while later, Dad arrived home. He stopped short when he saw Mr. Doherty leaning against our kitchen counter, sipping vodka and white lemonade while Mam sliced red and green peppers into strips. I continued to set the kitchen table, spotting Mr. Doherty's once-white tennis shoes covered in purple marker, a maze of small hearts. My scalp tightened. Ruth loved to doodle and purple was her favorite color. Dad excused himself. I watched his broad, blue-shirted back disappear.

"Do you like coconut milk, Mr. Doherty?" Mam asked.

"Dan, please."

She smiled. "Dan."

"I love coconut milk."

She poured the entire tin into the large, steaming saucepan, that dreamy smile never leaving her face. Ruth, leafing through the latest issue of *Jackie*, dropped the magazine onto the table and rolled up the sleeves of her blouse. She scratched both forearms simultaneously, their bloom of angry lines matching the red drag marks on her neck. "It's like scald on my skin. It's driving me mad."

Her shrill voice and exaggerated gestures would shame even the worst actors. I stared her down. She returned her attention to the magazine, her cheeks a hostile crimson. I got what she was trying to do, but her faking filled me with fresh, frantic suspicion.

Throughout dinner, Mr. Doherty told terrible jokes. "What did zero say to eight?" Next, he tried to impress us with trivia. What do you call a group of frogs? A group of ponies? Crows? We only knew some of the answers. When he asked how many windows are in the Empire State Building, Dad almost came out of his chair.

"Correct," Mr. Doherty said.

Dad's grin split his face, as if he'd just won big money on a TV quiz show. His eyes darted to Mam, hoping for approval. She was smiling at Mr. Doherty. I forced a goopy load of chicken curry into my mouth, the taste of coconut overpowering.

Mam offered dessert, the air thick with the drift of cloves and home bake from the oven. Mr. Doherty clapped his potbelly with both hands. "I really shouldn't."

"Nonsense. We have to indulge every now and then," Mam said.

Mr. Doherty chuckled. "True."

Dad's eyes paled to a lesser blue. He looked pained, as if some animal were lurking beneath the table, gnawing on his toes.

After bowls of warm apple tart and whipped cream, and too many cups of tea, dinner ended. "Say goodnight to Mr. Doherty, Triplets," Mam said.

"Goodnight, Mr. Doherty," we chorused.

"Toodaloo," Jimmy said.

"There he goes," Mr. Doherty said, and he and Mam laughed.

Mam closed the front door after Mr. Doherty, and held onto the handle for too long. No one mentioned his shoes with purple hearts or worried that Ruth might have drawn them.

That night, our parents' argument carried through our bedroom wall. "Maybe you could do with developing a bit of Ruth's 'don't come near me' condition," Dad said.

"How dare you! I can't enjoy some intelligent, interesting company? I'm not allowed to switch off and forget for a while?"

"You forget? What about me? What about what I need?" I could picture Dad's finger stabbing his chest.

"I've plenty more to forget about than you do."

While they raged, Ruth lay on her bed with her back to me. I stood over her, refusing to go away. "Tell me. How much is real, and how much have you been faking all this time?"

She sprang to her knees. "It's all real!"

"It's all in your head more like. *Oh. Oh. My shirt is burning me.*"

"Why would I do this to myself?"

"You're doing it to all of us."

"Leave her alone," Mary said from her bottom bunk, an authority to her voice I hadn't heard before.

I whirled around. "Tell her she's destroying this family. Tell her."

"Shut up and go to sleep, both of you. Isn't it enough that Mam and Dad are killing each other?" Mary dropped onto her mattress and pulled the yellow comforter over her dark head.

Stunned, I climbed to my top bunk and tried to sleep. I kept seeing Ruth's hand, working the marker over Mr. Doherty's shoes, drawing and filling in purple hearts—so many hearts, so much time and care, and all for a stranger.

⚭

Days later, Mary and I went for ice cream after school with a few of our classmates. We both felt guilty, knowing Ruth would be waiting for us at home, but our new friendships were a thrilling development we couldn't pass up. That was the real guilt: everything coming easier to us without Ruth's unsettling presence.

Just as we sat down, Mr. Doherty appeared at the café's window. He waved, flashing a brownish grin. I remembered the first day he came to our house, how he'd stained his leather jacket with his sweaty hand, leaving an oily print. The other girls asked who he was. Mary started to speak, about to kill the high mood and tell them he was Ruth's special needs teacher. I shoved the head of my ice cream into her face. She cried out, letting her cone fall to the table. She dragged the blue arm of her school cardigan across her eyes. "What'd you do that for?"

A couple of the girls laughed. Mary, tearful, dairy-eyed, swung her backpack onto her shoulder and charged outside.

Mr. Doherty watched Mary walk away, the sleeve of her cardigan still wiping her face. I thought about going after her but couldn't bring myself to move. If it had happened the other way around, she wouldn't follow me. So I stayed, trying to pay attention to what the other girls were saying.

When I couldn't stand it anymore, I went outside, just in time to see Mr. Doherty take off in his little red car, Mary next to him on the front seat.

A full hour later, Mary arrived home and swanned into the kitchen. "Where's Ruth?" she asked airily. Ruth was in town with Mam, seeing yet another doctor.

"Where'd you go with Mr. Doherty?" I asked.

"We drove all over, listening to music with the windows rolled down. I felt like I was in a film." She smiled to herself, one hand taming her windblown hair, the other reaching into the cabinet, removing the TUC biscuits.

I pressed her for details, but she wouldn't cave. "Fine, don't tell me."

Her bravado left her in a burst. "If you must know, he talked about Ruth the whole time, okay?"

"He didn't mention Mam?"

"No, nothing."

"What did he say?"

Mary rolled her eyes, much less hazel in her irises than in mine or Ruth's. "He thinks there's something extraordinary about her. 'Sacred' was his exact word."

It hit me that Ruth got all the attention for being the youngest and a misfit, and I got the odd mention for being the oldest, the first-born. But Mary was just Mary in the middle. Her thumb and finger touched the bridge of her nose.

"You really hurt me," she said. "And you also made me bang my leg against the metal bar beneath the table." She showed off the red bruise blotting her shin.

I fetched the tube of arnica from the drawer and dragged my chair in front of her. With my fingertips, I eased the lotion onto her coarse, stubbled leg. The room filled with the smell of licorice. I imagined she was Ruth and I was getting to touch her, to help her heal.

༄❦༄

The next week, I stayed home sick from school, my swollen tonsils an angry, white-spotted red. Mam set me up in her and Dad's room, afraid I might fall from the top bunk in my fever. Throughout the morning, I went in and out of a fitful sleep, awoken by the fire in my throat and heat in my veins. I rolled over on the damp bed, to reach for the glass of water on the nightstand. Mr. Doherty was standing over me. I cried out and jerked backward against the headboard, its iron scrollwork prodding my scalp.

He sat down next to my knees. I locked my legs together, as rigid and skinny as branches. "How are you feeling?" he said.

I tried to answer, but a volcanic rock was stuck in my throat.

"Can I get you anything?" he asked. I shook my head. "You sure? I just made your sister a delicious tuna sandwich." He smiled, a speck of celery caught between his top front teeth.

"No thanks," I croaked.

He touched the back of his cool fingers to my forehead. "You're burning up." I could smell his fish breath. He dropped his hand, and offered me the glass of water. "Drink."

"Poor Ruth," he continued as I drank. "To be beyond touch. It's almost impossible to imagine. She's like the sun."

After he left, the smell of fish lingered, the rank smear of creatures that shouldn't be among us. I didn't want Ruth to be alone with him. He was mesmerized while talking about her, that same shiny expression people got in church, praying before statues and burning candles. *Sacred*, he'd said to Mary. Yet he and Ruth had been alone together all these weeks and nothing had happened. It wasn't like he could touch her. And I had been wrong about the purple hearts. Mr. Doherty had decorated his tennis shoes, to get himself and Ruth started "on the right foot," he'd joked with Mam. My thoughts calmed.

Just as I was drifting off, a shiver passed over my back, like the fall of a cold, polyester slip. I sprang to sitting. Something was wrong. I could feel it in the fish air. I crept downstairs and through the kitchen, listened at the study door. Why close the door? I brought my ear to the cool wood but could hear nothing. From Jimmy's cage inside the living room, his metal swing creaked. No other noise anywhere, except my ragged breathing. I licked the salty sweat from over my lip, working up the courage to turn the handle. I burst into the narrow study space, finding it empty. Feeling watched, and ridiculous, I checked behind the door. I returned to the hall and searched the downstairs rooms. Just as I was about to go back upstairs and check our bedroom, I heard laughter carry from the back garden.

I peered through the kitchen window. The weather had turned, but despite the chill Ruth lay stretched out on the grass in coffin pose, wearing jeans and a white T-shirt rolled up to her ribcage. Her hollowed stomach and raised ribs made her look even more like a corpse. Mr. Doherty was kneeling next to her. "I give you the gift of the garden's touch," he said, his voice booming.

"Yes!" Ruth said, her back arching toward him.

He scooped up a mound of buttercups, daisies, and pink rose petals and rained down the bouquet on Ruth's bare midriff. She cried out in delight, her feet kicking and her hands clapping the earth. They laughed, the weak autumn sunlight glancing the tiny garden on her stomach.

I turned away and wrapped my arms around my waist, struggling to hold myself upright. A sharp ache filled my chest. Why hadn't I ever thought to do this for Ruth?

Outside, their laughter kept going off. My mind blazed with the sunshine lighting up the flowers on Ruth's naked middle, pretty, living contact that she should be enjoying with Mary and me.

⚮

I awoke in Mam and Dad's bed, my eyes swollen and stinging. I could tell from the dimness and the murmur of the TV downstairs that it was evening. Mam and Dad would be at work. I peeked out the window, confirming Mr. Doherty's red car was gone.

I found Ruth and Mary in the kitchen, looking into the freezer. I stopped in the doorway, fevered and shivering. Beyond the window, it was pitch black. Yet my eyes were full of Mr. Doherty's plucked bouquet on the grass, scattered now and dying.

"I saw you and Mr. Doherty in the back garden," I said to Ruth, my voice trembling, my eyes welling.

"You sound terrible," she said, pulling the box of choc ices from the freezer.

"Are you okay?" Mary said.

"Why'd you let him do that?" I said.

"Why are you being weird?" Ruth said.

"It was creepy. I'm telling Mam and Dad."

"No it wasn't. Shut up."

"Whose idea was it?"

"Mind your own business."

"Was it his?"

"So what if it was?"

Again that stab behind my breastbone, because I'd never thought to do it for her. "You know how much that would have meant to Mary and me."

"Don't bring me into this," Mary said.

"All these years I've begged." My voice cracked.

"Fine. We can do it tomorrow," Ruth said. She and Mary exchanged an exasperated look.

"It won't be the same." Tears and sweat stung my eyes and white dots buzzed midair.

"Come and eat some ice cream, it'll cool your throat, and your mood," Mary said, smirking with Ruth. They ripped the wrappers off the choc ices and placed the torn plastic in the bin. I felt like a third wrapper they'd discarded. The air inside the kitchen shimmered, as if infected with my fever—or maybe the swelter was rising off Ruth, the sun.

Jimmy called out, cutting through the haze. "Toodaloo."

"Hello?" Ruth said. "Mam? Dad? Is that you?" The silence ticked.

"Toodaloo," Jimmy said.

"What's got into him?" Mary said.

"Who knows," Ruth said, shrugging.

I moved into the living room and stared at Jimmy in heated wonder. The caged bird knew. He'd felt my leaving, and this scorched version arriving.

# INTO THE WEST

FINTAN SCANNED THE SPACIOUS KITCHEN and furnished deck beyond
the French doors, confirming everything was in order. A Tipperary
man, and raised in a two-up, two-down terraced house, he never imagined he would someday own such a fine home in a prime San Francisco neighborhood minutes from the ocean. He tugged on the cuffs
of his shirt and rubbed his hand over his silk chest, wondering if the
bold shade and tailored fit weren't too much? He glanced at the digital
clock on the oven. He had time to go change. But he looked good in
eggplant, and sleek. Blond, tanned, toned, and blue-eyed, he was often
mistaken for a Californian until he sounded his telltale brogue. The
doorbell rang. His eyes returned to the oven clock. Katie was early.

In the entryway, he thought he heard a key scratch at the front
lock. He imagined his wife, Liz, bursting through the door. A doula,
she was working the night shift and wasn't due home until morning—unless she'd gotten suspicious.

He pulled the front door open, bracing himself. Katie's arm shot
out, holding a bottle of wine. Her yellowed smile struck him again,
a relief from the sameness of Americans' pearly whites. Also notable
was her lean height—she was nudging six feet—and her long, tou-
sled copper hair, her lively brown eyes. He was doubly relieved that,
like him, she had dialed up her look: a black cocktail dress with a neat

bow at her waist, wrapping her like a present.

It was a warm, forgiving evening. Katie remarked on the orange-red sunset. They moved out to the deck and Fintan powered on the barbeque. They clinked wine glasses and faced the manicured garden. Growing up, his family's backyard was the size of a small rug. The line of deep green trees along the rear wall hid the neighbor's house, but they could hear the children playing hoops.

"Sounds violent," Katie said, smirking.

He chuckled. "How was your day?"

"I didn't save anyone."

"Lose any patients?"

"No."

"That's a good day's work, then."

"True."

He recalled the emergency room and his dislocated knee, an accident on the job and the worst pain he'd ever experienced—physically, at least. He remembered how her green nurse's scrubs added to her Mayo accent. How her face lit up when she realized he was Irish, too. How it hurt to laugh but he couldn't stop.

"And your day?" she said, her thumb wiping the smear of pink lipstick from her wine glass.

"Lots of pipe laid and we all survived the trenches."

"Excellent," she said, bringing her glass to his for the second time. "Now feed me." He busied himself with the grill.

They enjoyed dinner at the kitchen island, facing the garden, their knees sometimes touching. The meal finished, she glanced over her shoulder, her brow worried. "You're sure this is okay? I feel like I shouldn't stay much longer—"

"Relax. Liz is working all night. She won't be home until mid-morning." He poured more wine. It hit him that Mother's visit was three days away, another woman to add to the messy mix.

They kissed and moved downstairs. In the guest bedroom, they removed their own clothes, a spectator's sport. He lifted her onto his hips and dropped onto the king bed. She pushed him onto his back, her forehead already glistening. He shuddered with thanks.

⟨⟨⟨⟩⟩⟩

Fintan opened the front door, allowing Mother to enter the house first. She hesitated on the threshold, her hand pressed to the door-jamb. "Holy Mother of God, you could house an army in this."

"Hardly," he said, feeling a twinge of shame. She had visited him several times over the years, but this was her first trip since he and Liz bought the house last spring. He lifted her suitcase and followed her inside, turning to close the door and resisting the urge to rest his forehead against the dark wood. The entire forty-minute drive from the airport, she had complained about the flight. "A hostage, I was, for eleven hours straight, and with my knees up to my chin, the seats were that close together. There's rapists serve less time."

He was merging onto the 280 when she said, almost softly, "Liz never comes to meet me."

"I told you, she's working day shifts right now."

"You're both always working as far as I can tell."

She stopped on the plush floral rug in the entryway, taking in the large, window-bright living room, the curved mahogany staircase, the art-studded corridor to the kitchen, the second stairs leading to the lower level, and the gleaming dining table and chairs beyond yet another set of French doors. "Everything's bigger in America. It's pitiful."

He almost asked her to please not say anything like that in front of Liz—who was born and raised in Indy, Indiana and as all-American as high-fructose corn syrup—but Mother already knew the rules, and he already knew she would break them. "I'll put this in your room." He hurried downstairs with her suitcase.

She followed him into the guest bedroom, her speed unnerving. The woman was almost seventy and still as hardy as a goat. She sniffed the air. He cracked the window open, worried she could smell sex.

"You could swim in that," she said, gaping at the Jacuzzi tub inside the ensuite bathroom.

"Are you hungry?" he said.

"I don't know what I am."

"I'll make a pot of tea."

"Wait. I brought my own teabags." She reached for her suitcase.

In the kitchen, she deemed it too damp to eat outside on the deck (*Do you not get sick of that fog?*) and took her tea and roast chicken sandwich while standing at the window, admiring the back line of trees and colorful flower beds. He was eight again, watching her stand at the open front room window, pointing a shotgun at her husband and the father of her seven children. Dad was unfaithful, with a fresh-faced widow from Strand Street, and Mother wouldn't ever forgive him. Fintan's father wielded everything from threats to sweet talk to physical force, trying to get back inside his home. Mother fired the shotgun, twice. She never suffered another man again and raised Fintan and his two brothers and four sisters alone. All these years later that standoff was still the talk of the town, but Mother refused to be shamed. If anything she was proud. "No one will cross me again."

"Poppies," she said, voicing her first notes of approval since her arrival.

"I think so, yeah."

"You're not the gardener?"

"Pipelines, that's about the extent of my planting."

She laughed, and he wondered what else he could say to draw more of the same. "Liz then," she said, still smiling.

He admitted they paid a gardener to come twice a month. "I should have known," she said in a way that pulled at the bottom of his stomach. "You need to remember where you came from."

"Aren't I looking right at her?" he said, and they laughed. He told himself they just had to get through the next thirteen days.

He urged her to take a nap. "You must be exhausted." In fact, she looked a lot brighter than he felt. Her face smooth, eyes clear, hair bunched in a fist-sized bun, and her long, angular frame erect.

She pinched the face of her watch. "I might as well stick it out until bedtime."

He glanced at the oven clock, counting the hours, and of course she caught him. He clapped his hands together. "What would you like to do?"

"Have you wine?"

He thought to protest. Liz would be home soon and wouldn't be impressed. "Red or white?"

By the time Liz walked in on them, they had almost finished the bottle of cabernet and the entire wheel of Brie cheese, despite Mother finding the first too dry and the second too gooey. "Tastes like sheep. And the cheese is gamy, too," she'd said, making them both roar laughing.

"It's so good to see you again," Liz said, rushing at Mother.

Mother struggled off the barstool and tolerated Liz pulling her into a hug. He removed a second bottle of wine from the rack, uncorked it, and poured three large glasses.

"Goodness," Liz said, eyeing the potent measure.

They discussed dinner options and decided to order Indian. "I like mine spicy," Mother said.

"It won't give you heartburn?" Liz said.

"I know my own wants, thank you very much," Mother said.

Liz looked at him and drank deep from her wine. The takeout arrived. His lamb korma was disappointing, almost tasteless aside from the salt. Mother said "you Americans" more than once. He could practically see Liz's temper fanning out like flames.

Mother dragged a wad of naan bread over her plate, sopping up the last of the vindaloo sauce. "I was saying to Fintan that you both work too hard. Maybe if you didn't have this enormous house, you wouldn't have to. I've already gotten lost in it."

"I love this house," Liz said, managing to make it sound like an ultimatum.

Fintan opened another bottle of wine. Liz protested, but accepted a top up. About halfway into the third cabernet, the stilted conversation miraculously turned into a singsong. Mother started it, warbling along to Roy Orbison's "Crying" as it piped from the overhead speakers. The three took turns performing solos and duets, but mostly they sang together, his phone rescuing them from forgotten and mangled lyrics.

Mother raised her glass in a salute. "Now that's one thing Americans are great at—music!"

When she sang "A Bunch of Thyme," he was mindful of her wounds, her strength. When Liz sang "Me and Bobby McGee," he was sure he loved her.

After Mother went to bed, Liz rounded on him in the kitchen. "All she does is bitch."

"At which, you have to admit, she's superb."

"This isn't funny."

He followed her upstairs and into bed. They lay with their backs to each other inside the dark. He tried to conjure Katie and the other night, but kept seeing Mother sitting up on the guest bed, screaming that he was a cheat and aiming a cocked rifle.

"Like father, like son. That's what kills me," Fintan told Enda. He was in the lead, wading through a knee-high river of sewage below Fell Street, the beams from his helmet and spotlight sending hundreds of slick rats fleeing along the tunnel's sides, the light whitening their beady eyes and their squeals echoing. He raised the spotlight higher, illuminating the ceiling creeping with cockroaches. While he inspected the cracks in the animated, crumbling pipeline, Enda scribbled details of the damage onto a legal pad.

"The wife is going to find out sooner or later. They always do," Enda said.

After Mother shot at his father—she insisted she'd have hit him if she were aiming at him—Fintan didn't see him again until nine years later, when he tracked him down in London, on a building site in Brixton. His father, grayer, shorter, stood mixing concrete inside a large bucket with a stick. The entire time Fintan spoke, the man never stopped stirring.

"Is that it?" Fintan said.

His father glanced up from the thickening cement, his bloodshot eyes surrounded by pink, creased folds. "Is what it?"

"Right, thanks very much." Fintan walked away, fully expecting his father to call him back.

He remained in London another six months, also working the building sites, but when his father never came looking for him, and when every Irish person in the city was a suspected IRA terrorist amid frequent bomb threats and several deadly explosions, he cleared off. He headed for New York first, and eventually found his way to San Francisco and its kinder climate. Fifteen years later, and a part of him still expected his father to call after him; still expected to turn around and find his father's sorry face.

Fintan and Enda emerged from the manhole to the sounds of a commotion among the crew. Carlos was in the center of the group, pressing his phone to his chest and speaking rapidly in Spanish. Fintan understood enough to know there was something wrong with Carlos's daughter, and Fernando translated the rest. The five-year-old had fallen in the school gym and whacked her head. She was alert but en route to the emergency room. "Go on, get going," Fintan said.

"Gracias." Carlos wiped his eyes with the back of his hand and raced to his truck.

"You go with him, let us know if they need anything," Fintan told Fernando.

As the two men drove away, Enda said, "That's no coincidence, you know. At the end of the day, family's all that matters."

The week before Fintan left for New York, he saw his father in Leicester Square, walking with a slight, fortyish woman. Between them, a dark-haired boy aged seven or so, holding both their hands. At first Fintan thought he was mistaken, but it was definitely his father. He turned on his heel and followed the three as far as the Odeon Cinema. He hesitated while they bought their tickets, but continued into the cinema after them.

He sat several rows back, keeping the trio in his crosshairs. Throughout the film, his attention jumped between the screen and his father with his new family. More than once, his father's hand touched the top of the boy's head, shaking it gently. The child blindly swatted at the distraction, his eyes glued to the two boy leads, riding their magical white horse over the Galway hills. Whenever the audience laughed, his father's guffaw raked Fintan's eardrums. During a sad scene, when the boy's small hand wiped his tears, Fintan's father lowered his silvered head to the child's, his craggy profile loose and soft.

༄

Mother refused to walk across the Golden Gate Bridge. "I've crossed it how many times already?"

"It's not the same in a car," Fintan said. The woman had refused every suggestion for activities or sightseeing—whatever it took to occupy the time and give her a good trip. It didn't help his mood any that he was in withdrawal, unable to meet with Katie while Mother remained. The whole afternoon lay before him like a ledge, as did the next ten days of Mother's trip.

"We can do something else," Liz said agreeably.

"Our Sean was just a few feet out on that bridge when he had to turn back, said he was sure the wind was going to pick him up and throw him into the sea—"

Fintan recalled his oldest brother standing at the mouth of the bridge. Petrified, Sean was unable to move a limb or his speechless, bloodless head. Later, he laughed off the episode, but reeked of shame. It had spooked Fintan to see his big brother in such need of solid ground. He'd reassured himself he'd no such scars. Didn't he drop beneath the ground most days at work and tunnel through the earth?

"Sean said the noise of those speeding cars whooshing past and shaking the bridge—"

"All right. You don't have to go on about it. Forget the bridge," he said.

Liz touched his arm, and addressed Mother, laughing lightly. "I promise you, the bridge doesn't shake."

He moved to the cabinet, and the sink, and filled a glass of water. After several cold swallows, he was thrown back to the Odeon Cinema and that film, *Into the West*. An idea came to him. He glanced down, confirming both women were wearing pants and closed-toe shoes. "Good, you're already dressed appropriately. Just grab a warm jacket."

"I'm not going back to that Alcatraz. That place is polluted with ghosts—"

He herded the women into Liz's car, taking pleasure in keeping Mother in the dark about their destination and vexing her further.

When they entered Golden Gate Park, she said, "We better not be going to those Japanese Tea Gardens. You tried to get me there once before—"

"I swear if you say another word, I'm putting you out of the car," he said.

She chuckled. "Do you remember I used to do that to you kids? Sometimes you had to walk miles to get home. Yis weren't nearly as mouthy with the legs worn off yourselves."

Liz reached across the gearstick and squeezed his thigh.

"Are we going to that huge big museum again, the one with the white crocodile and the ceiling that showed outer space? I liked that," Mother said.

"'Huge big,' Fintan says that too. It's so cute," Liz said.

He could feel Mother's eyes roll in her head. She had never said it out straight, but he knew she was disappointed he hadn't married "his own kind."

Liz went on. "It's an alligator, actually. I always remember because albino also starts with 'a.'"

"We're not going to the Academy of Sciences, but good to know you like something," he said, meeting Mother in the rearview.

"Respect and manners. I like them."

She didn't speak again until he pulled into the horse stables behind the lake off Thirty-Sixth Avenue, home of the police department's mounted patrol unit. "What in hell?"

Fintan, Liz, and Mother strolled through the stable yard amid the stink of manure and press of fog and hay dander. Several horses stood at half doors, their heads looking out like question marks. The three stood cooing at the magnificent animals and rubbing their long muzzles. Fintan clapped the side of the white stallion's strong neck, admiring its name carved on a wooden plaque overhead. "Hello, Rusher." He'd heard tell of these stables over the years and had sometimes spotted the mounted police patrolling the park and downtown, and once in Fisherman's Wharf, but this was his first visit. He moved away from Rusher, promising to return, and immediately missed the warmth of the horse's body and breath, his huge eyes the color of wet acorns. He followed the signs to the stables' office, Liz and Mother in tow.

To his surprise, it was Liz and not Mother who caused a scene. "You can't spring this on us. I haven't ridden since I was, like, ten. What about your mother? You can't expect her to get up on a horse?"

"Why not?" he and Mother said together.

"Have you ever ridden?" Liz said.

"Yes," he said.

"You're a terrible liar," she said. He couldn't hold her gaze. *The wife is going to find out sooner or later. They always do.*

He requested Rusher. Mother wanted the brown mare, Maisy. Liz pleaded for the tamest horse in the herd. They suited up in rental riding boots and helmets. Fintan helped Mother, and then Liz, mount their horses. It took him several attempts to climb onto Rusher. Even their guide, Sasha, couldn't keep a straight face. Seated at last, he pushed back alarm at how far off the ground he was. Sasha repeated the rules and safety instructions, then led them out of the yard and onto a muddy pathway through the park. The three struggled at first, their tense bodies jerking on the horses, but they soon settled into a passable rhythm.

"I always wanted to try one of those mechanical bulls they have over here," Mother said, riding between Liz and Fintan in single file.

"I can so see you doing it, too," Liz said, laughing.

"Maybe once upon a time. It'll never happen now." Mother sounded wistful, almost fearful.

Rusher neighed and Fintan rubbed the top of the horse's head, overcome with tender feelings. "You're all right, boy."

Liz yelped. Sasha stopped on the trail and turned about on her horse, a braided pigtail falling forward. "You okay?"

"She started to go a little fast," Liz said.

"If she does it again, give a firm tug on the reins, let her know you're in charge."

"I should have put reins on my seven children, and my feckin' husband," Mother said. If Sasha heard, she pretended not to.

The four horses ambled on. For the second time that day, Fintan recalled the long-ago film. Like those boy actors charging toward the mythical kingdom of Tír na nÓg, he imagined galloping over the dark strand alongside the Atlantic's white waves, the sea and sky gray on gray and him urging Rusher to go faster, farther; to carry him clear off.

✺⊗⊃

Inside the brightly lit hospital cafeteria, Katie smothered her French fries in ketchup. Fintan tried not to look, he hated the sight of ketchup, but his attention kept returning to her plate. The line waiting for the food buffet was still snaking out the door. He should warn them off the chicken Kiev, crumbling like sawdust beneath his knife and fork. He tried to rally. What was wrong with him? He was with Katie at last.

It was the torture of being with her, but not *being with her*. San Francisco was such a small city—with spies everywhere, particularly among its large Irish community—he couldn't as much as hold her hand. Even this lunch was a risk, but at least if they were spotted here he would say he was appraising a job and ran into the nurse and compatriot who had fixed his gammy knee.

"I've a patient upstairs with a wired jaw who has more to say," Katie said.

He straightened on the plastic chair, laughing. "Sorry."

"What's going on?"

"Let's just say I'm now pronouncing mother mur-der."

She laughed. "From everything you've told me, I'd love to meet her."

He flexed a smile. At some point they would need to have a reckoning about what this was, and he didn't expect it to go well. *Ella es el mundo entero para mi*, Carlos had said of his little girl, who thankfully was fine after her fall. Fintan hadn't ever dared love anyone that much.

"I've lost you again." Katie's eyes chased him.

He was trying to work up to a witty comeback when a bald patient dressed in two gray-pink hospital gowns, one tied to her narrow front and the other laced at her bony back, drifted down onto a chair at the next table.

"Hello?" Katie said, dragging another French fry through ketchup.

The bald patient looked over, cradling a cup of steaming tea. She recalled a bare branch—her veins blue twigs, her eyes knots in bleached bark. A surge of terror swept Fintan up like the bucket of a digger. He leaned close to Katie, his voice urgent. "Is there someplace we can go?"

"You mean like a supply closet?" she said, laughing.

"Wherever." He winced, hearing how on edge he sounded.

"You're serious? Ew, no."

He gripped her wrist. "Please."

She pulled free. "Stop it."

He dragged his hand down his face. "I'm sorry, I..." He couldn't say that the forbidden somehow stopped the panic that came all the time now—ever since he'd gotten everything he'd thought he wanted in life, and it still wasn't enough.

"That's all this will ever be, isn't it? Stolen, secret fucks."

"What? No."

"What then?"

That digger in his head broke him up like road. He tried to form the words. She'd eased his pain, and made so much else fall away, too—but so had Liz, and the woman before her, and on and on. He wasn't ever going to fill up on it.

Katie rushed to standing. The untouched pear rolled off her tray and onto the floor. He reached for it as Katie moved away, its speckled green-gold skin torn, its white flesh dented. The bald patient remained at the table next to him, holding the teabag by its white thread and plunging it in and out of the water, as if repeatedly saving it.

It didn't seem like two weeks since Fintan had picked Mother up from the airport, and it also felt like an age. She jabbered in the front passenger seat, fretting about the long flight, the lines at the airport, and the stress of passing through security. "I swear, if any one of them uniformed fellas so much as tries to pat me down…"

"You'll be fine."

"I'd prefer to be mauled by a dog."

"Jesus."

"It's the truth."

To the best of his knowledge, no man since his father had touched her beyond a handshake. All this time, she'd remained married to herself, and dedicated to Fintan and his six siblings.

Liz had begged off the drive. "I've done my duty." She'd placed her hands on his face and kissed him, tasting of coffee. "No offense, but how'd you manage to turn out so great?"

The words sliced him. He silently promised her he would change.

Inside the international terminal, he waited while Mother dropped off her suitcase, his head full of the bald, emaciated patient. At death's door, Mother would say. He wondered about the young woman's regrets. Her wisdom. Her rage.

He and Mother walked to the security checkpoint. "Do you have everything?"

"Who has everything?" she said.

"Is a straight answer too much to ask?"

They stopped short of the boarding pass checkpoint. "This is as far as I can go," he said.

"Right so, son. Thanks for everything." She stretched up, placing her hands on his shoulders, and her brittle lips brushed his cheek.

"Mind yourself."

"Nobody else will," she said, laughing, and moved off. She flashed her boarding pass and the staffer, as short as a boy, waved her on.

"Mam," Fintan said in a burst. He hesitated, feeling choked. "Safe travels."

"Let's hope."

He watched her move along the dark line of passengers. Twice she looked back and he waved. She presented her passport and boarding pass. Placed her bag, jacket, and shoes on the conveyor belt. Moved beyond the x-ray machines and body scanners, and disappeared. For several awful seconds, he'd thought he was going to tell her that he'd cheated on Liz. But really, he'd called out to give her that moment of turning around and finding him still there.

# EVERYWHERE SHE WENT

INSIDE THE PUB there's the press of people and too-loud music. We get lucky and nab a couple of empty barstools, the cushioned seats still warm from strangers' bodies. We sip vodka sodas, his pale, freckled hand heavy on my knee. The wooden counter is littered with damp napkins, thin black straws, and drained glasses harboring soaked lemon slices and the remains of ice. Everywhere, drinks in various stages of disappearing.

He talks above the chatter and music, complaining about his day at the office, some trouble with a new employee. Hazel second-guessed him in a meeting, and in front of top management, including the CEO. My stomach tilts and my muscles grip my skeleton. He hasn't made the connection, has never given my Hazel much consideration. I suppose I don't say all that much about my best friend's disappearance at ten years old, but he should at least recognize this obvious trigger.

I have told him how Hazel's blue eyes made me want to go sky-diving. About her obsession with caterpillars, and what if they didn't want to change into butterflies? Her terror that her bellybutton would someday pop open. I've never talked about what might have happened to her when she disappeared—thoughts that have hollowed me out over the years and caused my eyes to sit too deep in my head.

I can't remember exactly the last time I was with Hazel. What we said and did together. Our parting words. All I have are scattered memories from those days and weeks before she was taken. Tiny films in my head that operate on automatic and flicker on and off. Flashes of us camping out in my backyard, pretending that tented patch of dirt was our very own island. Of our heads peeking from the tent's front flaps, finding fresh patterns in the stars. Of us tracing each other's faces with our fingertips, pretending to put on the other's makeup. Of competitions inside our school's dappled blue swimming pool, to see which of us could hold the other underwater longest.

"You're the only person I'd let drown me," Hazel said.

I had a lot more meat on my frame back then, rust-red hair, and chocolate brown eyes that over the years have lightened and turned evasive. Hazel's face and body were juts of bone like lookout points, and her hair was bark brown. To this day, her sky eyes hang over everything.

What I have no trouble remembering is the last time Hazel and I should have gotten together. She disappeared in the early afternoon, on a Sunday so hot the tarmac on our road bubbled. Hazel going missing on the Lord's Day, when the sun was at its highest and brightest, and while she was on her way to see me, still makes me feel as if I'm confined to an ICU at night—alone and tied up with tubes, everything dark and hissing, laced with static.

✺

Several nights later, he arrives home from work and finds me meditating on our bed. Even wearing headphones and an eye pillow, I can feel the ripples of disapproval he's radiating. He refuses to try meditation, claims he hasn't the patience. I'm new to the practice but am already a convert. When I focus on my breath long and well enough, I float, just like I did in the school swimming pool with Hazel. Brilliant colors explode in my head. A startling energy flows through and out from my body, as if I'm expanding beyond myself. Sometimes I drift too far and wonder why it was Hazel who was taken and not me. Think that if we were together, it wouldn't have happened, or we'd both have been stolen.

He stands at his side of the bed, his legs pressed to the frame, sending a little quake through the mattress. I remove my headphones and eye pillow. The light hurts.

"Is there dinner?" He drives his hand through his sandy hair, tiny flares of temper going off in his eyes. Different sparks used to fly between us, but they somehow cooled. He's not only annoyed that I was meditating, or because the apartment isn't pulsating with the aromas and heat of a homemade meal. Something else is needling him.

"What's wrong?" I say.

"Fucking Hazel. She thinks she knows everything." He tugs at the knot of his tie, all gasping force and wide gray eyes, as if the neckwear is crushing his Adam's apple. "I think she's shagging the CEO, too, so I can't touch her."

"Touch her?" I say.

"You know what I mean," he says, eying my bathrobe. The cool blue returns to his irises. "Are you naked under there?"

I unbelt the robe, knowing that in a better mood he'll be more obliging. I suddenly want to meet this Hazel.

<hr/>

The next day I show up at his office and offer to take him to lunch. He doesn't ask why I'm not at work. Usually, I can't bear to be away from my students, their eager spirits, malleable minds, and bracing straight talk, but today I phoned in sick. I lean over his desk and stage whisper. "Where is she?"

That groove appears between his eyebrows, like a coin slot in a vending machine. I realize there isn't anything I want to select from inside him.

"Hazel?" I say, still trying to sound playful.

He groans. "Don't remind me."

I follow him out of his office and watch his broad back while he struggles into his pinstripe jacket. He and the rest of management occupy glass offices that border the row of orange cubicles, as though they're about to ambush the subordinates.

I scan the scatter of employees, wondering which one is Hazel. I fantasize that she's my Hazel, and like me is now twenty-six. I can see her maze of bones, her forest hair and cloudless eyes. Reunited, we would cause a massive scene, flapping and shrieking like seals. I would have so many questions, and then turn angry, demanding to know why she'd left and stayed hidden.

He reaches the elevator and looks back, frowning. I slow-walk toward him, hoping someone will say Hazel's name or something else will give her away. The elevator opens and he gestures with his hand, indicating I should enter first.

My smile spreads to splitting. "Seriously? You're not going to point her out?"

"Why are you so interested?" Knowingness flickers over his face and his cranky look falls away. He appears almost contrite. "Hazel. Of course."

He's held the elevator doors open too long. The alarm goes off. Heads turn in our direction. I rush to the exit stairs. As I hurry down the bare concrete steps, he calls my name, but doesn't follow me.

Inside my classroom, the air is coated with the chemical smell of hand sanitizer which I apply often and liberally. Germs aside, I'm fond of my charges. My tender gaze runs over the rows of pubescent schoolgirls, every one a bull's-eye in this sick world.

I direct their attention to our history books, the chapter on King Henry VIII and the formation of the Church of England. I try to center the conversation on Henry's break with the Catholic Church, but my students only want to discuss the king's two beheaded wives. They blurt gory details about spurting jugulars and eyes blinking inside decapitated crowns.

"Crowns, get it?" Sylvia says, chuckling. She licks her lips, as though trying to get at the last of something tasty.

Sixteen years ago, there were elements to the horror of what happened to Hazel that some people also seemed to almost enjoy—a near exhilaration that it hadn't happened to them or their children, maybe. *There but by the grace of God. Wouldn't you love to know what happened?*

They liked to re-enact Hazel's last known movements, as if there was entertainment in trying to undo it. *If only someone had happened on the scene. If she'd stuck to the main roads. If she wasn't walking alone.*

They delighted in placing blame and assigning supposed fixes. *No one has the fear of God anymore. There's too much sex and violence on TV. We need more police. Bring back hanging.*

Some even held Hazel, or her parents, responsible. *Didn't she know not to talk to strangers? She should have fought and screamed. She was let run wild. What were her parents thinking, letting her out in a sundress the size of a hanky?*

"What about whoever took her?" I said. "What about what they should and shouldn't have done?" People looked at me funny.

A couple of nights after Hazel disappeared, her parents showed up at our front door and asked my mum and dad if they could borrow me. It still stays with me that they said that. *Borrow me.* I kept hoping someone was borrowing Hazel and would bring her back home soon.

Inside Hazel's kitchen, the smell of burnt potatoes bunched in my nose. Her dad sat me on his thick, fleshy lap. Her mum cried into the shredded tissues in her hands. "Tell us everything again," her dad said. "Everyone she knew? Everywhere she went?"

I couldn't give them anything useful.

Later, when I told my mum and dad they should never have let Hazel's parents take me, Mum hugged me to her lumpy chest. "Oh, chicken, we would never let anyone take you."

All that night, I couldn't sleep. No one can keep that promise.

⬯

The day he travels to Surrey on business, I return to his office. The receptionist, Sally, starts to tell me he's out. I interrupt her. If I don't ask for Hazel right away, I'll lose my nerve. Sally pulls a yellow pencil out of her dark, messy bun and uses its pink eraser to dial Hazel's extension. It's like the pencil is also stabbing me.

Hazel answers, and even through the receiver I can hear her accent is from Liverpool, not London.

Hazel and I stand face to face, shaking hands. She is blond, brown-eyed, muscular, and in her mid-thirties. Disappointment is a chisel. She's not my Hazel. Of course she's not. I knew that. I hold onto her hand for a beat too long and she peers at me, puzzled. I struggle not to bolt.

We take the elevator and drop through the building. My body rigid. My heart racing. Even my eyelids are damp. She doesn't seem surprised by my visit, or even curious. Seems to think I work for the company. She lifts her face, looking at the numbers over the elevator doors. We watch them light up and go out.

Over coffee, I repeat that I want to welcome her to the office.

"Are you HR?" she asks.

My face flames. "No, no. I'm an educator, and run training programs. I'm just trying to be friendly."

Despite her obvious relief, we grasp at small talk. I was hoping she might have something, anything, in common with my Hazel, and with me. I consider telling her the truth. She checks her phone and drinks her coffee too fast. Her trigger finger rubs the base of her nose. I should never have taken the afternoon off, leaving my students a second time for this woman, but the coincidence had glowed like a neon sign.

We exit the café. She gestures over her shoulder with her thumb, asks if I'm going back to the office. I don't meet her eyes, irises without a fleck of sky. We move off in opposite directions. A white plastic bag tumbles over the footpath toward me. The other day, on the Tube, a tourist said London has to be one of the cleanest cities in the world. The plastic bag clings to my feet and I have to do a little dance to free myself. "Unspoiled," the tourist said.

⌖

At home, during Sunday breakfast on the couch, my tongue works a raspberry seed from my top molar and I ready the words to finish with him. He won't be surprised. Won't put up a fight. He mentions an upcoming office party to mark his CEO's retirement. "My money says he and Hazel will run off together, and good riddance." He places his mug on the coffee table with too much force, splashing tea. "I don't know why I let her get to me so much."

He knows, I'm sure, but won't ever look that deep. I want to go to this party and get another chance with this second Hazel. I hold his head to my chest and smooth back his wiry hair, uncovering his entire ear. I remember Hazel telling me that owl's legs are long beneath all those feathers, and I refused to believe her. I don't ever get to tell her that now I know she was right.

He sighs and nuzzles his head against my breasts, as if falling into me. I get the feeling I could almost be good at taking care of others, but then it's gone.

❦

His company takes over an entire restaurant in Pimlico for the CEO's retirement party. Hundreds fill the glittering, sweating space, the men in suits and the women mostly skin. The live music drums my insides. The air wafts of garlic, seafood, and roasted meats. Trays of fizzy drinks weave through the crowd. Guests work the room like a runway and the dance floor like a contest. The other Hazel is wearing so many silver sequins they stick to my eyes.

I track her throughout the night, eager to reconnect, but don't manage to get close. Toward the end of the festivities, I follow her into the bathroom for a second time and finally we're alone together. I wait at the wall-to-wall mirror while she's inside a cubicle. She finishes, and joins me. We both paint our lips deep red. I imagine I'm coloring her mouth while she colors mine, like my Hazel and I used to do.

"Oh hello," she says in the glass, still holding up the gold tube of lipstick.

"Nice to see you again," I say, flashing a shaky smile.

She caps her lipstick. "You didn't tell me you were his girlfriend."

"Sorry about that. I know you two don't exactly get along."

"So what were you doing, spying on me?"

"No, not at all. It's complicated," I say haltingly.

She jabs the space between us with her bullet-shaped lipstick. "Keep away from me, you hear?" She hooks the straps of her snakeskin handbag onto the crook of her arm, making me think of Mum and a bygone era. Too much sends me backward.

After she leaves, I stay in the mirror, looking at my gaunt face and how my eyes look chased. Those old, choppy films flicker on in my head and the girl I was fills the glass. My Hazel appears next to me, and we laugh inside the mirror, all red, wet mouths and missing, innocent teeth. Hazel turns serious and stares at me, waiting.

"I'm sorry," I say. How many times will saying it, thinking it, breathing it, be enough? I'd ask her, but I'm alone in the mirror.

Later, in our bedroom, I tell him to sleep on the couch. "I can't do this anymore."

"What's gotten into you?"

"It's over. We're done."

"Are you drunk? You've been acting weird all night." When I turn away, he says, "Let's sleep on it, okay? We're both tired."

"Admit we're finished, can't you?"

His bleak eyes narrow. "You push everyone away."

"Get out."

"You're the reason we failed. You." His spittle hits my cheek.

"You make us sound like an experiment."

"For that, you'd have needed to be invested in the outcome. You never were, not really."

"Please just go."

"Not everything has to end badly, you know. Things can last." He bangs the bedroom door closed behind him.

The thud makes my insides jump. I feel rearranged, like all my parts have come together a fraction differently. I stand looking at the closed door. I didn't expect to feel anything. Didn't expect he'd have cared so much.

The day after I move out, I visit the Tower of London. Must be all the talk in my classroom of the Tudors. I sit on a bench beyond the Tower's tall stone walls, squinting through sunshine toward the Green where Anne Boleyn met her grisly end. The Tower is surrounded by a dry moat, its waterway drained years back and its circular hollow planted with grass. I picture the long-ago stretch of sparkling blue water inside the moat, and see myself paddling a yellow sailboat over the liquid void, to save Anne Boleyn.

I sit savoring Anne Boleyn's rescue. Then I imagine I track down Hazel's kidnapper and hold him captive inside the Tower's torture room. I whip him, lifting flesh from bone. Stretch and quarter him. Watch his severed head roll at my feet. It amazes me that victims' families and friends rarely exact revenge. How they can even sometimes forgive.

A thin blonde girl runs in my direction, her raised fists swinging, as if she's boxing the air. She stops in front of the White Tower and stands with her narrow back to me. I watch her, and the empty space beside her. My throat closes.

A woman, also thin and blonde, rushes at the girl. "There you are," she says, breathless, relieved. "Don't ever run off like that again."

"I want to make a wish, Mummy." The child's delicate arm swings out, and she throws a coin into the lush, green moat. It's as if she, too, can see the once upon a time band of water. The mother wraps her ropy arm around her daughter's shoulders and they remain still, as though waiting for the wish to come true.

When they move off, I take their place at the metal railing. My hand finds the cool coins inside my jacket pocket. I bunch the money in my fist and fire. The rounds of silver and copper fly through the air, not as barter for a wish to be granted, I decide, but in final repayment for any debts owed.

# Rare, But Not Impossible

MARGO ENTERED DUBLIN AIRPORT's arrivals hall alongside her fellow passengers, facing into the swell of waiting family, lovers, and friends. She looked away from the various emotional reunions, her throat thickening just as it had during the airplane's shaky descent, when she'd sighted the familiar patchwork of green fields through the window. Every time she returned, that first glimpse of home made her teary. She scanned the last of the expectant crowd, knowing no one was there to meet her and yet half hoping. Her parents were waiting for her at home—the trek to the airport too inconvenient and risky to their minds, its roads treacherous, its large roundabout lethal.

Shrieks sounded from the small group to Margo's right, another thirty-something daughter like herself back from New York. A watery-eyed family circled the willowy woman and clasped her inside thick arms sheathed in dark, rain-splattered vinyl, their voices full of the sunny weather that Margo wished was awaiting her. In the ten years since she'd emigrated, she had flown home maybe a dozen times, and every trip the sky spilled. She fixed on the exit doors and hurried toward the taxi rank. Inside the walkway's glass tunnel beaded with rain, her floral-patterned suitcase dragged after her with a scraping sound, its front splashed with a strip of red tape that warned *Heavy*.

⚮

Just once, Margo would like to not be grilled by Ireland's chatty taxi drivers. The gray Skoda had yet to hit the M50 and already Anthony, hefty and care-creased, had uncovered her pertinent details. Still, he wanted more. She reluctantly revealed she was a hairstylist—omitting that she owned a thriving salon in Greenwich Village—and was home for a friend's wedding.

"I hear the American accent now, all right." He laughed, a dog's yap. Margo suspected he went by Anto. She turned her head to her window, the rain still pelting. In recent years Dad had taken to calling her "the Yank." Her whole life, people criticized her voice— too posh for her Northside, working-class neighborhood when she was a girl; not Irish enough in New York City; and too American in Ireland. No matter where she was, she never sounded like she belonged.

She felt Anthony watching her in the rearview and kept her gaze trained on the lanes of speeding traffic to their right. Beyond the teeming motorway, a fresh crop of concrete buildings punctuated the endangered stretch of trees and fields.

Anthony's phone rang, a new, fancy Nokia with Internet. "Hiya."

A woman's voice tore the air.

"What do you want me to do about it? She's your sister," Anthony said. Another burst from the woman. "Stop letting her wind you up," he said. She continued her screed. "I've a fare, I have to go." He thrust his arm between the front seats, aiming the phone at Margo. "Say hello. She doesn't believe you're here."

"I'm here." Margo's voice came out thin and hollow. She was here, alone, her husband, Kevin, left behind in New York.

"Satisfied?" Anthony ended the call. "Sorry about that."

"It's okay," Margo said.

"I reckon the wife and her sister will kill each other one of these days. I'm rooting for the sister," Anthony said.

When Margo was young she'd longed for sisters and brothers, a big family. It was what her parents wanted, too, but Mam had hemorrhaged after delivering her and underwent an emergency hysterectomy. In her teens, Margo came to accept, and eventually cherish, her solitary standing in the family.

Anthony popped a toffee into his mouth and tossed its wrapper out the window. Margo swallowed a cry of protest, her head turning, watching the wrapper's flight. When she was nine or ten, she'd won her school's anti-litter poetry competition, her prize a hand-sized glass flamingo. The exotic bird was filled with pink liquid, and its color would magically drain and refill with a flick of the wrist. Her family, friends, and neighbors had marveled. "It was made in America," she said, impressing them further. It hadn't occurred to her until now that perhaps the flamingo was the first spark of America's pull. That, and her wanting a bigger life than what she'd had here.

✑⃝

Mam sat opposite Margo at the kitchen table while Dad remained on his armchair in front of the blaring TV, the sports commentator narrating a horserace with shrill excitement. Mam looked plumper, and Dad thinner, and both their faces were more lined. The kitchen, the entire house, looked much the same. Dad aimed his pen above the newspaper's racing forms, recording his wins and losses. He claimed he only ever bet pittance, but monitored each race as though he'd gambled his life savings.

"Eat up," Mam said, nudging the greasy, heaped plate closer.

Margo used to crave these staples from her childhood, especially the fat sausages and thick slices of brown bread slathered in butter, but she'd gone off fatty, processed foods in recent years and would much prefer fresh fruit and granola with a dollop of yoghurt. If she admitted as much, her parents would say she'd been living in America too long. She felt a little sick, her stomach out of whack from tiredness and the questionable airplane food.

"I'm full, thanks." She pushed the plate away, the two discs of black pudding staring up like large, empty eyes.

Mam ran her hand over her flattened, gray-brown hair. "I'm a holy show. I waited for you to come home to color it."

"I'll take care of it first thing in the morning. I brought the best of products."

"That's all right, I have my own stuff I like."

Margo swallowed the urge to coax. Her parents had never said it aloud, but they thought she'd gotten a bit big in herself in America. She felt the need to watch what she said around them, and everyone else here. To put herself down in good measure.

"It's a pity Kevin didn't come," Mam said for the second time. She and Dad loved Margo's husband of six years and had often congratulated her on finding a grand Irishman in America. "We wouldn't have wanted you to wind up with a foreigner."

"I told you he's busy at work, and the airfare's scandalous. Plus he has to come back for his brother's wedding in December."

Dad half came out of his armchair, goading his horse on. His bet won and he shot to his full height, his arms straight up in the air. He was less excited earlier when he'd met Margo and her suitcase at the front door. She recalled his rare hug with a warm feeling, his smell minty from the numbing cream he rubbed into his joints. He never failed to embrace her on her arrival, but it was a one-way gesture. The night before her departure, her parents religiously pretended they would see her at breakfast, but neither of them ever got out of bed to say goodbye. She supposed she also preferred dodging that pain.

She thought to phone the hair salon, to check in, but remembered the time difference. Over there, dawn was only breaking. She pictured Kevin in bed, her side of the mattress empty. Her head started to spin, faint from lack of sleep. "I'm going to lie down for a bit."

"You just got here," Mam said. She and Dad didn't understand jetlag, or appreciate the time and effort it took to get to them. Homebirds, they'd never travelled farther than England, and now, in the raw wake of 9/11, there was no way she was ever going to convince them to at last visit "the Big Apple."

As Margo climbed the stairs, Mam said, "She looks pale."

꧁꧂

Margo's childhood bedroom never changed—narrow, sparse, and a soft pink paint that coated even the ceiling. She was getting between the covers patterned with a field of buttercups when the telephone on the hall table rang. Even that sound was different in America.

Mam answered, her low voice carrying up the stairs. "She just went to bed, she's absolutely wrecked. Do you want me to go get her?" Kevin obviously said no, let her sleep.

Margo lay awake, fighting the urge to jump up and start punching the wall. After years of blameless service, her IUD had shifted out of place, rendering it useless. "Rare, but not impossible," her ob-gyn said. Margo could still see the pregnancy test stick, those two pink-red lines.

She and Kevin had never wanted kids. Their lives were full, rich. Margo booked an abortion. Kevin anguished.

"Maybe the baby's meant to be? Maybe fate is smarter than us?" he said.

"So you're going to fail me, too?" she said.

꧁꧂

Margo circled the supermarket's car park, searching for a vacant space while Mam fretted on the front passenger seat. "I don't like these new underground garages. All the rows and floors. Your dad can never remember where he left the car."

Margo spotted a parked van with its reverse lights on. She rolled Dad's Escort to a stop in the middle of the aisle and waited, shaky, fog-brained. She'd drank too much red wine at Brigid's hen party. Mam hummed nervously, loudly. The van rolled away, and Margo glided into the vacated spot. Mam jotted down the space's number and floor.

"I would have remembered," Margo said tightly.

Inside the busy supermarket, the noise and bright lights brought back the pounding headache Margo had woken up with. Janet Jackson's "Doesn't Really Matter" piped from the sound system. Margo, Brigid, and her brood of hens had danced and screeched to that same song inside the throbbing, neon-lit nightclub.

"You sound so American," Brigid's chief bridesmaid said at the start of the night.

"Doesn't she?" Brigid said, laughing.

When Margo admired a hen's designer "sneakers," the group snickered. At one point she almost said "mail" but caught herself. Some of the conversation was lost on her, notable Irish people and current events she wasn't familiar with. When she mentioned the taxi driver from the airport and his hot-off-the-shelf Nokia phone, the women said he was likely a gangland gangster. "A lot of the taxi drivers are now, loads of them big time into drugs and sex trafficking." The women hooted at Margo's shock. Throughout the night, she was careful to never sound like she was bragging. Twice, she was asked if she had kids.

Mam pushed the trolley forward and pointed to various items on the shelves, which Margo dutifully fetched. The trolley filled.

From another aisle, a woman shouted. "What did I say?" Slaps on bare skin and a child's wail sounded.

At the meat counter, Mam ordered four beef burgers and four chicken breasts. "Better to be looking at it than looking for it."

"Now you said it," the butcher said, his dark head the size of a football and his apron a brilliant, deceptive white.

At the line of checkouts, the same angry woman's voice sliced the air. "I told you to shut your mouth!" A thump followed, and the boy roared. A baby bawled.

Another woman spoke up, the stern voice of authority. "Is everything all right here?"

"She shouldn't be allowed to have children," Mam muttered. "Good people, on the other hand, should. Or there'll be none of us left."

As Margo drove out of the underground car park, Mam blessed herself. "We made it, thank God."

Sometimes Margo ached to move back home, and other times she was glad she lived on the other side of the world.

⌒⊗⌒

Margo and Kevin's mother sat opposite each other inside the picture-perfect living room, in full view of the rolling fields and their scatter of cows, trees, and houses. At seventy-one, Josephine remained an attractive woman with silver hair, a dewy complexion, and sapphire eyes. It was from her, rather than his late father, that Kevin had inherited his leading man looks. She wore a green and yellow plaid shirt over baggy brown corduroys, her wedding ring hanging from a gold chain that fell below her large breasts. Margo realized Kevin's father was dead three years already. It seemed half that length ago.

Her attention strayed to the upright wooden piano in the corner. She could almost feel its sun-soaked warmth. All these years, and she remained stunned that no one in the family could play the impressive instrument.

Josephine followed Margo's gaze. "I keep threatening to take it up one of these days. Meanwhile, I sit at it and pretend I can play." She chuckled. "It's almost as good as the real thing."

"How can you know?" Margo didn't ask. To her mind the neglected piano made for a sad ornament.

She accepted a second, cream-filled fairy cake, knowing she wouldn't be allowed to refuse. It was easy punishment. Josephine was an excellent baker and had given Margo many recipes over the years, but she had yet to try any of them.

"I'm a woman of leisure now. Niall and Jackie do everything about the farm, and do you think her expecting has slowed her down any? Not a bit. Niall did well there, I can tell you. As did Kevin," Josephine quickly added.

Margo pretended not to notice the slight. She always got the feeling her in-laws liked her well enough, but that she never quite measured up. "Do you miss the farming?"

"Not for a second. I served my time," Josephine said, laughing. She reached for the blue willow-patterned teapot and the wedding ring turned necklace dangled midair. "I'll make us a fresh sup."

Margo followed her mother-in-law into the kitchen. While they waited for the water to boil, Josephine gossiped about friends and neighbors who Margo either didn't know or could barely recollect. "You remember Elsie White from the post office? She died there a few weeks back. They're saying the kids buried her separate from the husband because at some point she had an affair. The names of plenty of suspects are flying about, but no one knows for sure. It's killing us."

Margo flinched. She could imagine what would be said of her, if they knew what she'd done.

Josephine nodded at the plant on the table, its pot still covered in green gift wrap. "I love orchids, thank you, they last ages."

Margo also appreciated the plant's resilience, and stark beauty. Plenty threw the orchid's skeleton away, but if you tended and waited long enough, the flowers returned, more striking on each bloom.

"You couldn't persuade Kevin to join you, obviously. I keep telling him he works too much," Josephine said.

"December will be here before you know it."

"This must be a very good friend of yours, that you came for her wedding?"

Margo bristled, hearing the accusation. "Yes. Brigid and I are best friends."

At least she and Margo were best friends growing up, and had managed to stay as close as could reasonably be expected, having lived three thousand miles apart for over a decade.

⁊⟨⊗⟩⊃

Back in the living room, afternoon surrendered to evening. Throughout, Josephine pressed Margo to eat and drink, and to tell her more news of her middle son.

Niall and Jackie returned home from the milk shed, their dirty wellingtons left outside the back door and their stockinged feet almost the same size.

"When are you headed back?" Niall said. Every trip, it was the question people asked the most.

Jackie rubbed her baby bump with both hands. "Four weeks to go. It can't come soon enough."

Margo wanted to cut Jackie's long brown hair into a shaggy bob with bangs and dye it pink-red, like rhubarb. It would open up Jackie's face and make her hazel eyes pop.

"You and Kevin need to hurry up and get in the family way, too. I'm not going to live forever," Josephine said, part jovial, part scolding.

Margo felt herself pitch forward toward the navy rug and blinking, inhaling, was surprised to find herself still sitting upright on the couch.

Margo's hosts insisted she stay overnight and not attempt to drive back to Dublin. "You could fall asleep behind the wheel," Josephine said.

Margo stuck to her plan. She was all talked and all quizzed out. The three thanked her repeatedly for visiting.

On the long drive home, the radio kept her company. She kept seeing Jackie. Even with that underwhelming hairstyle, the pregnant woman glowed.

The nine o'clock news headlined with Nelson Mandela's upcoming visit to Croke Park, to open the Special Olympics World Summer Games. Margo had vague memories from the eighties of a small group of young, working-class women, and maybe a lone male, too, who refused to sell South African produce in a protest against apartheid and Mandela's life imprisonment. The workers were fired from Dunnes Stores, and their resulting strike lasted years, until their jobs were finally reinstated and the Irish government banned the sale of South African goods nationwide. Margo didn't remember particularly caring back then, but now she appreciated those young protesters' strength and courage. To be ordinary and discounted, and to dare to stand up to that much power, it was risky, remarkable. It could crush you.

∽◌⟳

The next morning, Margo's parents scolded her for driving back and forth to Limerick in one day. "Madness," they chorused.

"I'm surprised the car had it in her," Dad said.

By evening, they were still going on at her over one thing or another. "That back door needs to stay locked," Dad said, forever fearful of break-ins.

Margo pinned her attention to the TV, yet another episode of the seemingly immortal *Coronation Street*.

"Josephine's grandchild must be due soon?" Mam said.

"Sometime next month."

"Is that her first?"

Margo's face burned. "Yeah."

"That's exciting." Mam glanced at Dad.

He straightened on his armchair. "You do realize—" He sounded like he was about to impart some agreeable but vital wisdom. "That our family line will die out if you and Kevin don't get a move on."

Margo stood up and left the room.

"You didn't have to put it like that," Mam said.

"What did you want me to say?" Dad said.

Her parents had made many such comments over the years, Mam mostly. *How much longer do your dad and I have to wait? Yis are trying, aren't you? Have yis had yourselves checked? What do you mean you're not having any? That's not natural.*

Each time, Margo hit back harder. She'd thought by now they knew better.

Mam knocked on Margo's bedroom door and poked her head in. Margo pretended to search through a dresser drawer. They sat together on the edge of the bed of buttercups. "Did your dad and I do something wrong? Is that why you don't want kids?"

"No, of course not. Why are we even talking about this?"

"Are you afraid you won't be a good mother? Because that's nonsense—"

"No—"

"Kevin, then. Is he the one—"

"God, Mam, stop."

Margo had interrogated herself often enough. She didn't need Mam drilling her, too. She liked kids well enough, and loved her godson, Finn, but she hadn't the slightest maternal urge.

"Something's wrong, I can tell. Maybe a child is what's missing?"

"I mean it, stop." If her parents ever found out she'd gotten an abortion, they would never forgive her.

Mam raised her hands, her lined palms facing out. "All right, fine. But I'll never understand you modern women and your wanting to do everything differently."

Margo's hurt and anger softened. Mam couldn't ever concede that the church and state had played and cheated women since time immemorial. It would call into question her entire existence.

"And I know there's something you're not telling me," Mam said.

"I'm okay, I promise. You don't have to worry about me."

"I hope not."

"You know I love you, right? You and Dad." The country had entered an era where such declarations were allowed, even practiced.

Mam's chin quivered and her hand jumped to the side of her dyed head. "My hair's going to go to hell again when you're gone."

⊱⊰

The phone rang. Margo was home alone and almost didn't pick up, afraid it was Kevin. To her delight, it was Teresa, her best friend in

New York and a fellow immigrant, from Edinburgh. "Can you talk? How are you holding up?"

Margo dropped to sitting on the bottom of the stairs, the mustard carpet thinning, blackening. "I'm all right."

"No one there knows?"

"God no." A fresh wave of dread washed over Margo. Kevin might tell people here, out of spite or the need for support.

"And physically?"

"Yeah, fine. A bit achy and nauseated the past couple of days, but nothing compared to how I was."

"Kevin called me. He said he phoned a few times but he hasn't heard from you."

"I need to call him back."

"I think that's a good idea."

"Can we talk about something else?"

"Yeah, of course. Sorry."

Margo told Teresa how she'd driven over two hundred and fifty miles in one day. How she poisoned herself with red wine the night of Brigid's hen party. How she'd remembered the glass, liquid-filled flamingo she'd won.

"For what?" Teresa said, amused.

"My anti-litter poem. *Don't be rash. We'll move your trash. Don't be a mug. Don't be a litterbug. Put it in the bin and we'll collect it then.*" How easy the solutions had once seemed, how clear right and wrong.

"You still remember it," Teresa said, laughing.

"Of course. For years that was my claim to fame."

"Speaking of, I stopped by the salon a couple of times. All's well."

"You're very good, thanks. Yeah, I've been on to them every day. They're flat out." She'd owned the salon for three years and still worried it was too good to be true.

Teresa told Margo how already New York was so humid she was melting. How their friends Tommy and Gina had gotten engaged. How she'd walked the Brooklyn Bridge for the first time. How her husband Miles had gotten his fancy work promotion. "Sometimes I can't believe this is my life now. Like how did I get from there to here, you know?"

Margo had known, before her IUD betrayed her. "You haven't mentioned my godboy. How is he?"

Teresa spoke in a rush, as if she'd been bottling up all talk of her son, for fear it was too soon and sore a subject. "He drew himself and a dog inside the moon. Guess what he wants?"

Margo smiled. Finn was a gas little fella, and his raven-haired cherub face was itself a work of art.

She and Teresa spoke for over an hour. Then Teresa needed to go pick up Finn from preschool. "You and Kevin will get through this. I know you will."

"Yeah, thanks, bye." Margo replaced the warm, damp receiver, her ear still tingling with its memory and her head full of her poem about collecting waste.

⚭

Inside the packed church, the entire congregation was white. The great number of people of color in New York City was the biggest culture shock when Margo first moved there—that and the fast-talking hordes, frantic speed of life, incessant beeping horns, and the sky-piercing high-rises. Now, with Ireland's influx of refugees and immigrants, it was the segregation here that she found striking, and disappointing.

It struck her that God might not want her in His house, a supposed sinner sitting in one of His pews. He should have designed people better, then. Orchestrated our biology so that sex couldn't ever lead to an unwanted pregnancy.

The organ music started, sending up the wedding march. The two bridesmaids slow-walked up the aisle, splendid in blush pink and with yellow-faced daisies peeking from their updos. The flower girl followed, carrying a basket of pink rose petals. Brigid's mother, dressed in electric blue and with a matching oversized hat, walked her daughter up the red carpet, both women radiant. Brigid smiled straight at Margo. Margo's finger swiped the outer corners of her eyes.

After the ceremony, outside the sunlit church, people said the happy couple was blessed with the weather. Overhead, a flock of swallows, fellow migrants, sailed past, their split tails unmistakable.

❦

The wedding dinner moved on to dessert and the speeches. The best man admitted he'd also fancied Brigid way back and commiserated with her for making the wrong choice, drawing raucous laughter. Next up was Brigid's father, who rambled to an excruciating degree, even getting in mention of his gout. Brigid also took to the microphone. It was less what she said and more how she looked at her new husband that made Margo's skin prickle. Margo was afraid she would never again look at Kevin like that, nor he at her.

After the meal, the hotel staff cleared several dinner tables from the plush function room, freeing up the wooden dance floor. In the lag time before the band started, Margo wandered the hotel's colorful gardens, glad to be alone. She knew several of the wedding guests, chiefly Brigid's family and a gaggle of old friends and classmates, but she felt shy and awkward around them after so long apart. The evening sun warmed her head and shoulders, and the surround of flowers and trees soothed her.

A handbell rang, summoning guests back to the function room. Margo obliged, steeling herself. The band called the bride and groom for their first dance. Margo watched the beaming couple, Kevin's absence like a hole cut into the air. She downed her glass of champagne, only half registering its fizzy sweetness. Seven years earlier, she had accidentally found her engagement ring inside one of Kevin's dress shoes. She promptly proposed to him, so as to maintain the element of surprise. They opted to get married in Ireland, to make everyone happy. They honeymooned on a small boat, sailing the Shannon and needing to be rescued by the Coast Guard when a night storm over Hodson Bay caught them unawares. Ever after, their terrifying near deaths made for a great story. How they'd gripped each other like buoys as the raging winds and heaving waters battered the boat. How they'd told each other at least they would die happy.

Margo waited until the first dance was over before going to the bathroom. Inside the cubicle, she discovered bright pink blood on her underwear. She remembered the liquid-pink flamingo, appearing full or empty with a tilt. This was her first period since she'd ended her pregnancy. Hers and Kevin's. He had supported her, accompanied her, but admitted he didn't know if he could ever make peace with it.

The bathroom door banged open. Margo could see the flower girl's white shoes and ankle socks beneath the cubicle door. The child skipped across the black and white checkered tiles. Margo emerged and moved to the metal dispenser on the wall. She fished a euro coin out of her handbag and inserted it into the contraption. The steel knob turned with a clang. The sanitary product dropped with a soft thud. When she turned around, the flower girl's keen gaze zeroed in on the tampon in her hand.

She bent down to the girl's level. "Hi, I'm Margo. What's your name?"

"Samantha." She pointed at the tampon. "What's that?"

Margo hesitated. "It's a special plug."

"I need to go!" Samantha cupped her crotch with both hands, balling up her white tulle skirt.

Margo pressed her hand to the child's narrow back and guided her into the nearest cubicle. "Do you need help?"

Thankfully, Samantha was already tugging down her underwear and hoisting herself onto the toilet. Margo returned to her cubicle and remained inside long after Samantha exited and others came and went. She sat bleeding, shedding. She wished she had said something more to Samantha, about women having a superpower that could also be a curse. Both of which we should have full reign over.

Margo arrived home drunk. Her favorite part of the entire wedding was going up to the bridal suite before the cake-cutting ceremony and refreshing Brigid and the bridesmaids' updos.

"You're a pure artist," Brigid said, admiring her hair in the gold-framed mirror.

"Mighty altogether," the two bridesmaids said.

Margo's mood lifted. This was her way of creating, contributing, and it meant something.

Her parents, long gone to bed, had left the hall light on for her. The rest of the house was in darkness.

She dropped onto the bottom of the stairs and phoned Kevin. "I'm not calling to talk. I don't want either of us to say anything."

"Um, okay." He sounded confused, but compliant.

She leaned her head against the wall, her eyes closed. She pictured him sitting alone on the couch, in front of the paused, silent TV, his free hand maybe on the cushion next to him, inside the dent her body had made.

They listened to each other breathe.

The night before Margo's departure, inside the warm, brightly lit kitchen with its lingering waft of shepherd's pie, she worked up the courage to say goodbye to her parents.

"Won't we see you in the morning?" Dad said.

"You know you won't," Margo said, ending the long tradition of pretense. It would be one less lie among them. She kissed Dad's sunken cheek and hugged him.

Mam was crying even before Margo reached for her. "Maybe you'll come back in December with Kevin?"

"Maybe," Margo said.

She walked upstairs to her room, an anchor around her neck. In an ideal world she would have her life in America here, and for her parents' sakes she wouldn't be an only child.

In bed, she recalled the piano in Kevin's family home. She pictured Josephine sitting at it, shrouded in sunlight and pretending to play. She placed her hands on her sides, her fingers tapping her ribcage like white keys. Her eyes filled at the harmony in the silent music, and at the surprising alliance. She and Josephine, both had made peace with not using a sacred instrument to its supposedly highest purpose.

# UNWANTED

EVERY SUNDAY AFTER MASS, I parted ways with my family and hurried straight to Bob's Bargain Bookshop, my fifty-pence pocket money tight in my fist. It was 1980, in Dublin, and I was a black-haired, dark-eyed, fourteen-year-old runt of a lad. On a flush week, I'd also have my takings from refunds on the glass bottles I collected out of the bins and lanes around our neighborhood, empty, sharp-scented treasure. Our locale was also home to Midas's gambling arcade, Mountjoy Prison, Cross Guns snooker hall, Luigi's chipper with its snapping, popping Pac-Man machine, and the reek of the Royal Canal.

Occasionally, I stole money from Da's hiding spot under the inky, floral carpet beneath his bedroom window to add to my dismal funds for books, comics, sweets, cigarettes, and cider. I only ever took a pound or two at any one time, knowing not to get greedy or careless. Amazingly, Da, who was skint, miserly, and forever howling about the cursed recession, never seemed to notice the missing money. I sometimes worried he was playing a game, waiting to catch me in the act and pounce. Then he would demand his pound of flesh, like Shakespeare's Shylock. *If I can catch him once upon the hip, I will feed fat the ancient grudge I bear him.* Da was forever reciting that bit with alarming passion—fist on his heart, glitter in his blue eyes, and an actor's boom to his voice—but he never seemed to be aiming the Bard's words at me.

Each Sunday, I spent hours browsing inside Bob's Bargains, rifling elbow deep through the discount bins and scanning the shelves of book spines, their jagged top lines like broken horizons. I bought as many used mysteries as I could afford, and sometimes sprang for a brand-new book that I couldn't bear to delay reading. I sped through every adventure of the Famous Five, Secret Seven, and Hardy Boys, and especially loved the Agatha Christies. Hercule Poirot? Bleeding brilliant. What I liked most about the best mysteries was not being able to figure out how things were going to end. Too many people around me seemed to think they knew exactly how everything—their lives, the world—was going to end, and it was rarely good. I preferred to keep my options wide open.

Those dizzying shelves of colorful books never failed to lather my already voracious appetite into a near frothing frenzy. I'd feel mad tempted to shove books down the front and back of my jeans, but I could never muster the courage. Thankfully, my best mate Charlie knew no such limits. The rare times the opportunity presented itself, Charlie, his hair shaved of all its blond and his face freckled and fleshy, stole the most popular new books and gave them to me. New-new, like. With that tree smell, smooth, crisp pages, and must-have stories fresh from the publishers. Those were the best books, the ones everyone wanted and that Charlie took for me.

For my fifteenth birthday, Ma gave me two green leather-bound hardbacks, *Frankenstein* and *The Great Cases of Sherlock Holmes*. The old, pored-over books had belonged to her da. My fingertip traced the faded, flaking gold ink on their covers and spines, my touch reverent, fluttering.

While both classics warmed in my hands, Ma—her air distressingly casual—announced that Doyle's Corner, the crossroads up the street from our house, was named after Sir Arthur Conan Doyle himself, the creator of Sherlock Holmes, the greatest sleuth of all time. Stunned, I demanded to know why she hadn't shared this nugget of local history long before. She knew I had my own sights set on becoming a detective, and the more brilliant and famous the better.

Da looked up from the newspaper and called Ma's claim a load of nonsense. Red spilled from Ma's purple-webbed cheeks into her forehead and down to her wrinkled chest. Da said Doyle's Corner was named after the real jewel in its crown, Doyle's Public House. Those Doyles of the publican persuasion, Da insisted, were a bloodline as far removed from that dead knight and Protestant bastard Arthur Conan Doyle as you could get.

"I'm telling you, Doyle wasn't a Protestant," Ma said, livid. She tried to collect herself and smile at me, but the curve of her lips refused to stay in place. "Your grandda loved those two books," she said, a wobble in her voice.

My four grandparents died before I was born, a mixture of the cancer, bad luck, and heinous crime. By all accounts I was most like my Ma's da, our curious heads constantly in books and make-believe. Poor Grandda had met a savage end, mugged and beaten to a pulp with a hurling stick, and for pittance. He didn't die until three years later, but everyone blamed his untimely death on that unmerciful battering, saying he was never the same afterward. His as-good-as-murderers were never caught. That would all change, though, as soon as I finished school, joined the Guards, and turned detective. I would reopen Grandda's case, scrutinize his police reports, re-interview suspects and witnesses, and chase down new leads—all with the same flair and ceremony that Da brought to his Shakespeare recitations. Whatever it took to solve the longtime mystery and finally bring Grandda's vicious assailants to justice.

I read *The Great Cases of Sherlock Holmes* three times. Every now and then I would pause on the page, thinking with a pleasant shiver how Grandda had been here before me, reading these same sentences and holding this very cover. The book's introduction stated Arthur Conan Doyle was a Scotsman and a medical doctor, and even fancied himself as a bit of a psychic. There was nothing about him being a Protestant.

"Didn't I tell you," Ma said to Da with the same relish she usually reserved for a fat, oozing slice of Victoria cream sponge.

"None of yis know anything," Da said.

The book's introduction also stated Doyle came to hate Sherlock Holmes and eventually killed him off, only to later bring him back from the dead. I wished I could bring Grandda back.

It took me a while to get around to reading *Frankenstein*. I'd no interest at first. Really, I only liked mysteries. Ma kept asking, though. "Your grandda claimed he was never the same after reading it," she said, that shake back in her voice. When I did finally relent and give the book a go, I devoured *Frankenstein* too, reading and re-reading for such long stints my eyes burned and my neck and shoulders ached. It seemed to me that all doctors wanted to play God, but Frankenstein wasn't content to only save lives and resuscitate the dead. He took his grandiose urges to the last precipice, desperate to create a fully formed being of his sole making.

Like Doyle, Frankenstein also came to hate the creature he'd brought to life. All that made me think of Charlie's ma, Agnes Owens. "I curse the day yis were born," she told Charlie and his older brother, Jim, spitting like boiled water.

Ma said Grandda reckoned Doctor Frankenstein and Sir Arthur Conan Doyle saw too much of their flaws and weaknesses in the men they created and it terrified them. Agnes didn't see herself in her boys. And she most certainly wasn't afraid of them. I had deduced it was actually the opposite. Jim and Charlie weren't nearly enough like their creators for Agnes's liking. She wanted her two boys to be as savage as their parents and to take her side against their da, the dreaded Archie Owens.

Archie was balding, tight-jawed, and small-toothed. He also harbored a vampire's need to break skin and draw blood, especially that of his wife and two sons. Months earlier, he'd beaten Charlie to such a state I hardly recognized him. For ages afterward, a film played on repeat in my mind: I kick in the Owens' front door and drag Archie from their smoky, yellowed kitchen and out onto our falling-down street. I knock the brute to the ground with a smack of a crowbar to his limp-haired head. His scalp splits and blood pops like pus from a pimple. Agnes stands at their front gate, cackling. Charlie and Jim remain in the front doorway, as still and unseeing as statues. I keep going with the crowbar 'til Archie is a mess of shattered bones and red, quivering pulp.

Thoughts of pulverizing Archie the way others had destroyed Grandda made a fist squeeze my guts and twist. Another kind of guilt rushed in. I could never do in real life anything close to what I did in that imagined scene. I couldn't avenge Charlie. Couldn't even protect him. To put the film and feelings on pause, I fast-emptied a flagon of cider into my head.

✸❦✸

When I wasn't collecting used glass bottles, stealing Da's money and Ma's cigarettes, or hanging around with my gang of gurriers, as some people insisted on calling us, I was ever on the lookout for new mysteries to solve. Usually, my caseload consisted of little more than lost dogs and cats, the theft of milk deliveries from our neighbors' front steps, and figuring out which boys were riding which girls. Then, al-leluia, I landed my biggest case ever.

Charlie's older brother Jim didn't come home one Saturday night, or on the Sunday, or the Monday. Where had the seventeen-year-old gone? Had he made his great escape, as Charlie claimed? Maybe he'd immigrated to London for work, like most of the coun-try's young? How far could he have traveled, though, without mon-ey or supplies, and how was he faring for clothes, food, and shelter? Charlie insisted Jim would get himself sorted someplace and then come back for him.

Two months passed with no trace of Jim. Charlie seemed to give up on ever hearing from his brother again. "Good riddance," was all he said now. Then he'd kick at the curb, or a car tire. I made inquiries, but despite my best efforts, no one wanted to talk.

Jim's mott, Bernice, was a whisper's reach of sweet sixteen and already going around with some new fella. When I asked them about Jim's whereabouts, they laughed—man-tits whooping like a pigeon and Bernice sounding like the crack of snooker balls colliding. She seemed reason enough for Jim to do a runner, never mind his ma and da.

Liam, Jim's supposed best friend—with his woozy eyes, twisted teeth, yellower skin, and permanent smell of glue—proved to be as helpful as Bernice. "What about Jim?" he said. "He's gone, so long, move on." I plied him with questions, but to no avail. "Get out of here," he said, "or you'll be on the missing list, too."

In a stroke of brilliance, I decided to make posters, similar to those Old West WANTED ads. I even went so far as to offer a reward for any information that would lead to Jim's return. Maybe the grand total of five pounds wasn't much to some, but to me it was a small fortune. It amounted to weeks of saved pocket money and refunds on bottles, and getting greedy about fleecing Da. It also meant no new books for a while. It was worth it all, though, to give something this big back to Charlie.

I set out one dark, cold evening, my breath a tiny fog and the stars rips in the sky. I hurried over the streets, armed with superglue, a staple gun, and the ten original posters I'd handmade, all done in different colors with pencils and markers. I climbed telegraph poles, lampposts, and even the giant oak tree across from our school. Despite the chill night, I enjoyed a warm thrum in my chest as I worked, picturing the grin on Charlie's face when I reunited him with his big brother.

✑

The next day, Charlie caught up with me as I walked home from school. He was only eleven months my senior, but he'd left St. Vincent's the previous year, having barely passed the Group exams.

"What the fuck did you do?" His fist hovered my face, one of my MISSING posters balled up in its grip.

The two lads walking alongside me scarpered. Charlie mashed the round of poster against my lips. I tasted blood, sweet and sharp. When I spat, the red glob foamed on the ground. I hoped it would bubble in Charlie's brain forevermore.

He pulled pieces of torn posters from his various pockets. "I found six. How many more are there?"

Wings of panic flapped in my chest. "What's your problem?"

He swung at me, but I pulled clear. I didn't have time to feel triumphant. He flew at me, knocking me backward to the footpath. He straddled my chest and slapped my head with his open hands, supersonic left-right smacks. He was red-faced, heaving. White froth simmered at the corners of his mouth. His eyes had darkened, rage drawing almost all of the green out of the brown. My shouts mixed with his grunts and the sounds of alarm and protest from onlookers.

Hands pulled at Charlie, flashes of freckled, cracked, and nicotine-stained fingers. A dark blue vein bulged in the center of his forehead. He got another few slaps into me. I pushed up from beneath him and poked my two fingers into his left eye. He fell backward, roaring. I scrambled to my feet, pushed through the circle of gawkers, and hurried home, hurting in a way that had nothing to do with my ringing ears and throbbing face.

The next evening, our neighbor, the widow Harney, appeared at our front door, her mouth downturned and her eyes lasers. We didn't have a phone at ours, so I'd put her number on the MISSING posters.

Inside her hallway, I stopped next to the mahogany phone table, taking the smallest breaths I could—the air tainted with what I hoped was only the smell of boiled eggs. Mrs. Harney entered her living room, leaving its door ajar. Her rope-thin shadow on the wall placed her right behind the door, her woolly-looking head cocked toward me, and the television beyond her on whisper.

"Hello?" I said into the receiver's black, pitted mouthpiece.

"I'm answering your poster," a boy's harsh voice said.

"Yeah?" My heart tugged upward.

"Meet me tomorrow night, nine o'clock, in the lane behind Ulster Street."

"Who—"

He killed the call. I held onto the receiver, anticipation coursing through my veins. Charlie was going to feel like a right prick when I brought his brother back, and he would steal a whole library of books on my behalf to make up for clattering me.

The following night brought a thick darkness, the slice of moon a dappled silver and the stars nothing but pinpricks. I got a bad feeling as soon as I turned down the lane behind Ulster Street and walked deeper into blindness and the tang of stale piss. I could barely see beyond my hands, and there was something about the silent, seeming emptiness that made me doubt I was flanked by the usual limp litter, clumps of weeds, and empty bottles at the lane's edges. Gone, too, was the sense that there were houses on either side of me with their back gardens full of grass, trees, hedges, and flowers, all the life that could still thrive when winter was mostly without mercy.

Just as my gut screamed at me to turn and run, bodies—one, two, three—rushed me. An arm collared my throat, a stranglehold so strong it pushed my Adam's apple deep into my neck.

"Where's the money?" Moist lips brushed my ear, making me shudder.

"Get off me." I struggled, all shoulders, arms and legs. Glass smashed, and the bulk of a broken bottle sliced the night close to my face. The serrated stump pressed my cheek. Every time I blinked, I felt its teeth.

The first fella spoke again at my ear. "Do you want to lose your eye over five pounds?" His breath smelled of cider, and something sharper. Maybe his own insides.

I pulled my knee up, about to ram my heel into the neck of his ankle. One of the two lads in front kicked my shin. I bit down on my lip to gag my groans, my mouth still puffed and tender from Charlie's beating. The third fella searched my pockets and patted down my body and legs. From my right sock, he pulled out the cylinder of five one-pound notes I'd rolled with such care. He drove his fist into my nuts. I doubled over, my air exiting in a burst.

The three boxed, kicked, and thumped me so many times, the blows turned to almost music. I thought of Grandda, robbed and beaten to near death, and wondered if he'd also made a symphony of the repeated fall of that hurling stick as it broke his bones, his scalp, his teeth.

Fingers grabbed my hair and pulled back my head. That damp, sweet-sour breath hit my face. "Nice doing business with ya." The broken bottle ripped through my cheek, hitting bone.

I dropped to the ground, my head smacking the concrete between two red suede shoes. Six spindle legs packed into black drainpipes ran off into the night. I had just been battered, maybe to death, by three Teddy boys. Even in my state, the idea galled me. Teddy boys were made for dressing stupid and break dancing, not for smashing up people, and most of all not a future brilliant detective. The fools had left enough clues for even a bad investigator to track them down. I swore, if I survived, I'd see them serve time, and the longest sentence possible. As I went under, a terrible thought seized me. Maybe Charlie had put those three Teddy boys up to this, instructing them to finish what he'd started.

❧

I woke up in the Mater Hospital, Ma, Da, and my three sisters gathered around my bed. Ma sat in a chair to my right and Da stood opposite her to my left. They were both holding my hands. The edges of my sisters' eyes looked raw and sore, and when they saw my eyelids peel back, their mottled faces lit up like little bonfires. Cold fear gripped me. I had to be dying. That thought, and the jaundiced glare of the ceiling lights, hurt my head. I closed my eyes again, for days.

The next time I woke up, Charlie was leaning over me, his grooved face hovering. He jerked upright, his cheeks turning a scalded red. "Fuck. You scared me."

While I tried to get my mouth to work, the spooked look left him and his demeanor returned to hard and cocky, as if even his insides weren't wet and soft.

"Don't worry, I didn't kiss you," he said.

"Wha?" My mouth felt stuffed with a wad of gauze and my throat hurt, as if its lining was scraped raw.

He smiled. "Lying there all this time like Sleeping bleeding Beauty."

"Yeah, well, it's not like you could break the spell. You're no prince."

"You're no beauty," he said.

I chanced smiling and cried out in pain.

"Are you all right?" he said.

"Do I look all right?"

"You look woeful."

"This is the one time you pick to not tell a lie?"

He laughed. "On the bright side, you've never looked better." His hands moved to the front of his khaki army jacket, and he pulled its zipper up and down. I watched the silver teeth open and close, open and close. In my head, the broken bottle rushed again at my face. My hand jumped to my cheek, flinching at the feel of the nylon stitches and the swollen, tender ridges.

"Do you know who we have to thank for the improvements?" he said.

I tried to read him, to tell if he already knew exactly who had done this. "No," I said, stalling.

"You must have seen something."

My head filled with the red suede shoes and black drainpipes. I hesitated, not sure if I could trust him. What if he was fishing to see if I could identity my attackers? If I was going to rat to the Guards and testify against the Teddy boys, and him?

"You didn't recognize a voice, or anything telltale?" He looked wretched, his face pale and creased, his eyes dull and glazed. But still something wouldn't let me shake the suspicion he was the master-mind behind it all.

"Nothing."

"You're lying," he said.

"What do you care? You practically killed me yourself."

"Yeah, sorry about that." His eyes slid away.

"What *was* that?"

"Just drop the whole Jim thing, okay? He left, so let him stay gone."

"Okay, fine," I said, relenting. All along, I think I'd known what he could never say out loud. That Jim was dead to him ever since he'd taken off and left Charlie alone with their parents. But I'd cared less about what Charlie wanted and more about solving my greatest mystery yet.

"I wish they'd done it to me and not you."

I'd never heard him sound so full of feeling. Despite my pain and the fog of medication, my mood soared. He hadn't set those Teddy boys on me.

"As soon as you get out of here, we're going to find whoever did this and we're going to mess them up, slowly, massively." His hands curled around my metal bedrail, his pale knuckles threaded with red. The specks of green in his eyes seemed to spin. "They'll pass out squealing."

My heart beat against the bars of my ribcage. He was serious. I returned to the memory of him straddling me on the footpath and whaling on me, out of his mind with that certain hunger. Charlie's ma was wrong. She and Archie had made at least one son in their likeness. Something inside me flipped over, crushed and smoking. I was always so caught up with everything I wanted to uncover and solve, I'd never thought about the things I was better off not knowing.

# COLLISIONS

THERE WERE THOSE WHO classed Sheila and me as two auld lesbian drunks—we'd heard the sneers over eons—but we were more like very sociable sisters. That afternoon, we'd taken up residence in our usual corner nook inside Clancy's. Outside, the downpour ricocheted off places and people.

"The doctor reckons it's irritable bowel," Sheila said. "Of course Fergus said I've irritable everything."

We laughed and a few of the men at the bar turned their squashed, cranky faces. We had watched the same sad cases sitting on the same barstools for almost three decades, the need and the sourness rising off them like the stink from the nearby Liffey.

"The gas is the worst of it," Sheila said. "What's the polite word for it nowadays, flatulence?"

"Fart-u-lots," I said.

We hooted, and the men scowled harder. Rain rattled the windows, as if trying to get in.

⌇⊗⌇

The TV hung on the opposite wall. The regulars bitched about Clancy being too mean to get a plasma widescreen. These days most everyone wanted the latest, greatest gadgets, and the bigger the better. Sheila and me liked the small TV and for things to stay the same.

The TV presenter, head tilted to the left as if that side of his brain was heavier, claimed that two moons had once orbited the earth. Both moons collided, scientists now believed, and merged into one. Hence the two sides of the moon are different, the presenter continued, with one side mountainous and the other flat and full of craters.

The talk on the TV turned to the presidential election. Photographs filled the screen like mugshots, a lineup of those hoping to become the next token head of Ireland.

"The state of them contestants," Sheila said from behind her glass of vodka and diet Coke.

"I don't think they're called contestants."

"Well they should be," she said, setting us off again.

"Shut up, you annoying hoors," Decker Dicey roared from his high stool, his short legs dangling midair like a child's.

"You tell 'em, Dicey," Moanin' Nolan said.

The protests of the rain addled windows weakened to a shivery whine. Clancy came out from the counter and added coal to the fire, his back hunched and arse aimed.

"They're saying that's what's killing the ozone layer. Holes as big as continents," Sheila said.

"I heard that, all right. Still you can't beat the open fire," I said.

As a child, our house had three fireplaces, with only the one in the living room in use. The two in my parents' and brothers' bedrooms were boarded up, the cost of fuel too much and the draught from the chimneys an icy spirit. There was something about my parents' fireplace in particular, maybe that the hummingbirds on their bedroom wallpaper put me in mind of flight, but I was convinced that behind the wooden boards and red bricks there lay a secret passageway, leading to someplace magical.

"It's that long since Fergus and I did the business," Sheila said. "It's like I've me own hidden tunnel."

We laughed. Then Sheila quieted. "I miss not missing it, you know?"

She always got a bit maudlin around the six o'clock hour when Clancy would be fixing our third drink. Sure enough, she closed her eyes and tilted her torso from side to side.

"Ah stop now," I said, knowing what was coming.

Sheila's voice floated out, eerie and practiced, like a seer at a séance. "I don't know how my poor Ma did it, blind and with six children. Too proud, she was, for a white cane. Too stubborn. Nothing but the darkness and the terror of putting one foot in front of the other."

A chill stole over me, like putting on damp clothes. All these years and I still hated to sleep in an empty bed in the dark.

"I think that's what killed any longing left in me," Sheila said. "The fear that I'd get caught again after the fourth. I couldn't have coped with any more. Would have gone downhill as fast as Ma. Her mind sank as quick as the Lusitania after the sixth. Even with two good eyes, children will best you, let me tell you. And once you go off the sex long enough, sure you lose interest in it altogether, don't you?" Her hand clapped her mouth. "Ah, jaysus, sorry. Listen to me going on to you of all people."

Way back, I buried my third and final husband. I lost the first to leukemia, the second to a fall from a roof, and the third to electrocution while he was fixing a blown fuse. Clancy carried down our drinks and two packets of dry roasted peanuts. Sheila and me would always get an awful craving for a salty, crunchy snack at about that hour. For the first time—and I don't think I imagined it—the peanuts stung going down.

As the bells of the Angelus tolled, Clancy's front door creaked open. Every head turned. A tall, skeletal youth entered, bringing in the rain and wheeling a neon orange bicycle. In place of the cyclist's left leg stood one of those stick metal jobs. He leaned his bicycle against the far wall, removed his matching orange helmet, and approached the bar.

"All right to park her there, sir?" he asked Clancy, his American accent too soft for any of the east coast states.

Clancy's eyebrows struggled to life. "Yeah, grand, at least until the evening rush."

The men parked at the counter snickered. We were the evening rush.

"How can he cycle with that contraption for a leg?" Sheila said.

"Where there's a will," I said.

The American ordered a toasted ham and cheese sandwich and the homemade vegetable soup that was out of a tin.

"Give the gentleman fresh bread and don't skimp on the ham," Sheila shouted to Clancy. She smiled at the American. "He thinks he can get away with toasting the stale stuff."

"I'll thank you to mind your business," Clancy said, swaggering to the back kitchen.

The American raised his hand to the brim of his imaginary hat. "Thank you." He looked at me. "Ma'am."

Sheila and me grinned. "I know you Americans like big portions," she said. Two of her sons had emigrated to New York, and she often threatened to bring me along when she finally visited them, but neither of us was much for breaking with routine.

Sheila patted the black, fake leather seat next to her. "Come on over here, can't you?"

"Run, Yank, run," Decker Dicey said.

"Shut up, you,' Sheila said.

"I think I'll just..." The American swerved, making for the table next to his orange bicycle.

Sheila pounced from the nook and grabbed his arm. "You're all right." She fired her raised voice straight at Decker Dicey. "We only assault our own."

The American was born and raised in Iowa, a farm boy, and had spent the past three weeks cycling the jagged edges of Ireland.

"There's men with two legs wouldn't do what you've done," Sheila said. "My Fergus, for one. He wouldn't walk, let alone cycle, from the couch to the fridge, even if he was famished."

Amusement honeyed the American's irises and my breath caught, remembering my first husband. The last Sunday of every month I visited each of my husbands' graves and always stayed the longest with Joseph. He had that same shimmering gold in his eyes, like the throats of the hummingbirds on my parents' bedroom wallpaper.

Clancy reappeared with a steaming white bowl. We ordered another round. The American agreed to a pint of Guinness. He sipped and slurped the imposter soup.

❧

Sheila and the American traded story after story. We laughed so hard Decker Dicey complained he had ringing in his ears. The American claimed that his false leg drew the girls like a celebrity, and admitted he delighted in fabricating tall tales about the real cause of his injury. Instead of the actual culprit—the stab clear through of the prong of a forklift—he told girls the leg was blown off in a mortar attack in Baghdad. Or that he was a professional motorcycle racer and had lost the limb in a blazing, multiple bike pileup. In one of his more far-fetched, but no less successful offerings, he'd contracted a flesh-eating disease, forcing surgeons to amputate.

"You must think women are horrid stupid?" Sheila said. His grin fell.

He looked straight at me and ended the silence with, "You're very quiet, ma'am?"

Sheila, her face looking emulsified from the vodka, leaned over the table toward him and stage-whispered. "Very sad. She's a widow three times over." She turned her bleary eyes to me. "Aren't you?"

He rubbed the back of his fair head with the flat of his hand. "That sucks, ma'am. I'm sorry."

"We call her the Angel of Death." Sheila laughed, a single shot.

His gaze darted to me, alarmed, sympathetic.

"I've been called worse," I said.

Sheila suggested more drinks. He refused. Sheila coaxed and then bullied, seeming to forget he'd caused offense, but he wouldn't be swayed. He returned to the rain and we returned to ourselves, the mood dulling in his absence. I pictured him gliding over the slick Dublin streets on his bright orange bicycle, maybe thinking of better, more honest stories that he could tell.

Sheila and me watched the nine o'clock news in silence—more reports of the world spinning out of control.

A half-hour after closing time, Clancy demanded everyone finish up and get out. Sheila and me ignored him, sipping and savoring. Soon, though, there would be nothing for it but to struggle up from the nook, put on our coats, arm our umbrellas, and amble home. Sheila had Fergus. I had the cat.

Sheila closed her eyes and rocked to and fro. Her forefinger traced a circle on her left palm as she recited the all-too familiar nursery rhyme. "All around the garden went the teddy bear..." When Sheila was a child, her mammy would trace Sheila's palm while singing the same rhyme and then walk her fingers up Sheila's arm and tickle her armpit. Save for the tickling, Sheila had performed the same ritual on her mother as the blind woman lay dying.

Sheila wept, drawing more creased looks from the last of the men at the bar. I urged her to finish her drink, any hope of getting her out of Clancy's with a semblance of grace diminishing by the second.

"The hands are rich in nerves, did you know that?" Sheila said, her finger still going round her palm.

"So is the face," I said, remembering back forty years and Joseph's thumb caressing my lips.

⁊⊛⊃

Outside, Sheila and me struggled over the wet footpath arm-in-arm, our shoulders knocking against each other. I stopped and looked up at the distorted sky and melded moon, my eyes blinking against relentless rain.

We'd told the American about the possibility of two moons once upon a time. "Amazing that they didn't destroy each other when they collided," he said, raising his glass. "Those moons are two survivors, just like you and me."

No one had ever toasted me. Not like that.

"Come on, what are you at? We'll be drowned." Sheila pulled me after her toward home and I allowed myself to be led, going slow, slow past the dripping buildings and streetlamps, a corridor of burning lights.

# At the Side of the Road

Cissie Murray sold Wexford potatoes and strawberries by the dual carriageway, under a gray-white awning she pretended was a fancy marquee. For every hundred cars that passed, maybe one stopped. Meanwhile, Cissie held hard to her phone—texting friends, playing games, and bopping to music with frantic rhythms. For this, Dan Topher paid her thirty euro a day.

This Friday, Cissie had forgotten her phone at home. She felt clammy and irritated, her hands, her head, having little to do. For hours she hummed songs to herself, watched greenflies race over the strawberries, and haggled with a few customers, all wanting something for nothing.

Shortly after noon, just as Cissie was thinking about doing handstands to feel her blood run, a blue Honda Civic pulled up. Right off, she could tell the fortyish driver wasn't interested in her potatoes or strawberries. He strutted toward her, a gummy, twitchy fella with a bloated face and mad, dilated pupils.

"What's a grand little thing like you doing all alone at the side of the road?" His Drogheda accent sounded like something broken. He leaned closer over the dirty potatoes, looking like he was about to demand a bag full of her. She gave silent thanks for the table of produce between them. He reeked of fermented sweat, and his brown, rotted teeth made her think of a dilapidated fence.

"You must get right bored, like? I know just the cure." He grabbed his crotch and his cracked tongue darted from his face. Cissie grabbed the golf club she kept by her nylon chair and raised it high with both hands, trying not to betray the shake in her arms. He whirled about and rushed to his car. Cissie dispatched a roar that felt fantastic.

✺

Mid-afternoon, the rain beat down on Cissie's fantasy marquee. In three hours, she hadn't made a single sale. She could see her mother's smug, jellied face. The whole country was down on its knees with the recession, and still her mother singled her out for failure. At least she had a summer job to get her through until September, and then she didn't know what. Her parents were insisting she attend college ("They let you in, didn't they?") but that seemed like another cage. She could emigrate. Only that didn't feel like a choice, either, but more like her generation's sentence.

The endless vehicles plowed past in the spiteful rain, sending up a dirty spray. The constant going, everyone else in motion, made Cissie feel as if the downpour had gotten inside her. She imagined waving her arms at the traffic, as though she were in some state of emergency. A young, muscular man would pull over in a shiny car, looking tanned and gorgeous, or else pale, chisel-faced, and with just the right amount of edge. He would sample the strawberries and invite her to taste the juice coating his thick lips. Right there, on the grass verge, they would fuck until he shattered everything that had numbed inside her.

All afternoon the July rain drummed the awning, the heavy, black clouds determined to sink the entire island. Near evening, a certain strawberry caught her attention, one shaped like a tiny heart.

"Aren't you lovely?" She looked around, feeling foolish, but only the cows in the fields and crows on the power lines could have overheard. She placed the strawberry inside one of the countless white plastic bags beneath her stand, and then into her backpack. Later, at home, she would dip the strawberry in sugar and disappear the fruit heart with the barest nicks of her teeth, in full and languid control of its erasure.

Dan Topher's battered white Hiace appeared in the distance. Cissie felt sick to her stomach.

"Is that all you sold?" Dan would roar, his eyes so wide their lids seemed taped back. "Are you good for nothing?"

Only it wasn't Dan behind the wheel, but one of his field workers, Trevor. A looker and maybe a year or two older than Cissie, he could have stepped out of one of her daydreams.

*⚬⚬*

The Hiace rattled down the motorway toward Dublin, Cissie so rigid with temper she seemed all bones. As they'd packed up, Trevor had thrown her tent into the back of the van like it was nothing. That pretend marquee was the best part of this whole gig.

Trevor sat smoking a roll-your-own cigarette. She could taste the blue-gray smoke. She coughed, putting her whole body into it, but his only response was to cut a smirk. In the rearview, her mood made her brown eyes inkier. The rain had darkened her hair, too, plastering it to her head, and her mascara bled black down her face. She would look a lot prettier if she fixed herself, but forget that.

Trevor caught her looking at his hands, dirty from picking potatoes and strawberries all day long. The Hiace picked up speed. Usually Cissie craved any kind of thrill, but she didn't much care for racing in this rain, not with the blinding mist coming off the heavy traffic in front. They barreled over the slippery tarmac, the van's rattle growing. She pressed her foot to the floor, biting back a plea for him to slow down, refusing to give him the satisfaction.

Trevor lifted his phone from between his thighs and started to text.

"Put that away," Cissie said, no longer caring about her pride.

His thumb continued to type, his attention jumping between his phone and the road. The van's noises climbed, the sounds of falling apart.

"Stop it, I'm serious," Cissie said.

He laughed. "Relax."

Just as she was about to slap the phone from his hand, an articulated truck swerved into their lane. "Watch out!"

Trevor slammed the brakes. A wet squeal. Cissie lurched forward, the seatbelt locking hard against her chest and neck. They wobbled for several long, chilling seconds. The van righted itself.

"You okay?" Trevor asked.

"What do you think?" she said, rubbing the side of her neck.

"Calm down, would you. There's practically fumes coming off you." He lifted the last of his cigarette from the ashtray, inhaled with a hissing sound, and issued a series of smoke rings. Cissie followed the float of circled smoke toward the ceiling. She imagined wearing the breathy bracelets on her wrist, still warm from his mouth.

At the edge of the city, the Hiace passed the shell of yet another ghost housing estate, each unfinished home a headstone to the collapsed economy. Cissie's hand remained clasped to the side of her neck. It didn't hurt any longer, but Trevor didn't need to know that.

"I'm going to this concert in town tonight. Kacey Musgraves. Do you want to come?" he said.

"She's American, right? Country?"

"That's the one."

She started to say no. She didn't like Trevor or country music, didn't have her phone or much money, and was soaked head to toe. "Yeah, maybe."

In town, inside the food court next to the Academy, Trevor sneaked extra food for Cissie from the all-you-can-eat Indian buffet. She enjoyed a warm, giddy feeling as he spooned the rice and meats onto her plate, an illicit two-for-one meal. The chef, intent on his work and oblivious to their theft, stood skinning a gnarl of ginger root. He worked the peeler backward, drawing it toward his body instead of away. Cissie saw a flash of him peeling a strip of skin from his hand. She wondered why he'd put himself in unnecessary danger like that, just as Trevor had earlier. People needed to be more careful with themselves, and others.

She ate fast, barely breathing, barely chewing, the spicy flavors singing in her mouth. Once she'd sated the worst of her hunger, she slowed down, holding the curried food on her tongue, savoring. Trevor watched, his face shiny and lips greasy. He seemed almost aroused. She allowed herself to linger for a beat on his fall-into-me eyes, his let-me-drink-you lips.

She hadn't been with a fella in ages, not since Derek. After eighteen months together, Derek dumped her. "It's gotten old, you know?"

No, she didn't.

"Why Cissie?" Trevor asked. "Do your parents not like you or something?"

"I used to know another Trevor."

"Oh yeah?"

"Yeah. We called him Not-So-Clever Trevor."

His smile snapped like a rubber band. "Aren't you hilarious?"

On the street, Cissie and Trevor waited in the long queue outside the Academy. Passersby stared, there something about a crowd and the fear of missing out.

"Who's playing?" a youngfella asked the attractive couple standing in front of Cissie and Trevor, his Dublin accent sharp enough to gouge.

The woman, likely Polish, replied.

"Who?" the youngfella said, the single word a deep stab.

The woman nudged her companion's arm. "You say."

Cissie wanted to have someone in her life that she could tell, "You say."

Trevor continued to text. Cissie's fingers twitched, missing her phone.

"Gina's here. Nice." Trevor scanned the long queue of concertgoers. Someone called his name. He lit up, his smile pushing back his ears. A pretty, lean brunette squeezed her way through the waiting crowd.

Trevor and Gina hugged. "What are you doing here?"

"You mentioned you were going and I thought what the hell." Her eyes cut to Cissie and back to Trevor. "I'm not interrupting anything, am I?"

He laughed. "God, no."

Cissie's cheeks burned. "Absolutely not."

"Nice to meet you," Gina said, reaching for Cissie with both arms. Cissie pulled free of the shocking embrace and scanned Gina's face for malice. She found none.

⌇⊗⌇

Inside the Academy, amid the crush of people, Gina pulled two white plastic cups from her bag. "Sorry," she said over the piped music. "I didn't know you were joining us or I'd have brought a third cup."

"That's okay. I didn't know I was joining you, either," Cissie said.

Unfazed, Gina handed Cissie a cup and fixed Trevor with a dopey smile. "Trevor and I can share." She poured a small amount of Coca-Cola from the bottle peeking from her bag. Next, the head of a liter of vodka appeared. She filled both cups to the brim.

A burst of theatrical smoke clouded the stage. The audience clapped and cheered. Cissie had never heard of the support act, a young, bearded duo from Alabama. She took a long drink, the alcohol setting fire to her throat and chest. Gina kept fixing Trevor with that smile, and touching his arm, pressing her hand to his lower back. Cissie's jaw hurt from gritting her teeth. She was in their way. Unwanted. She took another long drink.

As Kacey Musgraves sang, Cissie swayed to the music, telling herself she was sexy, happy. She stretched her arms overhead, her thin, pale limbs ribboning the air while the singer crooned about the misery of trailer parks, and following your arrow wherever it points. Then one line cut too close, making Cissie feel as if more rain was falling inside her. *Same hurt in every heart.*

A heaviness came over Cissie, worse than if her roadside tent had collapsed on top of her. Derek had reached inside her chest and pulled out some tiny, essential part, dimming the rest of her. She could have died in the van earlier with Trevor, and she wasn't sure it mattered all that much that she hadn't.

ঙ⬭ঙ

Blinking, unsteady, Cissie exited the Academy, trailed by Trevor and Gina. She was headed in the opposite direction and made her goodbyes.

"You sure you'll be all right on your own?" Gina asked.

"Yeah," Cissie said, the music and vodka still coursing through her. She almost told Gina about the pervert earlier. How she'd chased him off with a golf club and her roar, stopping another man from hurting her.

"You enjoyed it," Trevor said, triumphant.

Cissie startled, then realized he was talking about the concert. She scoffed. "Anything's better than your driving and our near-death experience."

"What?" Gina said.

"Come on, you know you'd do it all over again," Trevor said, his dimples like finger pokes in dough.

"What are you two talking about?" Gina said.

"You couldn't be more wrong." Cissie wouldn't ever give him another chance to scare her, risk her.

She walked away, heading for O'Connell Street. People milled about, laughing, shouting, and others like Cissie keeping it all in. Yellow and red car lights sliced the night. Cracked tires blasted spray from rain puddles. Stars riddled the black. The moon was a bandage.

Cissie stood alone at her bus stop, remembering the strawberry. *Same hurt in every heart.* She eased the plastic bag from her backpack, wondering if Derek ever thought about her. The strawberry, lying on its side on her palm, no longer looked like a heart but the head of an arrow. *Follow your arrow wherever it points.* The fruit's head was aimed at her. What was that supposed to mean?

Her bus arrived with a screech. She climbed the stairs inside the double-decker, turned right instead of her usual left, and dropped onto a window seat up front. She rushed the strawberry into her mouth, tasting a seedy mix of tart and sweet. As she ate, her determination gathered. She'd survived twice in one day, and she was going to make that matter to the fullest. She looked through the fogged glass at the damp, twinkling city, and down at the pedestrians dotting the street, the lot unable to keep up with the bus, with her.

# BLINDSIDED

MRS. HENNESSY STEPPED OUT onto the road, pushing a polka-dot pram. Dave, the school traffic warden, rushed forward, his stop sign raised. The toddler inside the spotted contraption was blond and sky-eyed. Mrs. Hennessy was dark-haired and night-eyed. She must be at the babysitting now. With the recession, most everyone was willing to do just about anything to get by. Look at him, a qualified carpenter, reduced to a lollipop man for St. Brendan's School.

He stood guard in the middle of the crosswalk as Mrs. Hennessy sashayed past, ignoring him entirely. He wasn't much of a talker. But she could at least have some manners. "You're welcome," he muttered.

He only knew her last name. He'd heard the schoolchildren address her as they trailed him and his stop sign across the road, more of a jeer than a greeting in their young voices. The woman, middle-aged like him, was sexy, brazen, in her tight-fitting short skirts and hourglass figure. Even he, a confirmed bachelor, couldn't help but get caught up in her allure. This particular morning, Mrs. Hennessy looked and smelled especially mighty, a scent that suggested roses and a generous pinch of pepper.

Dave stared after her, admiring the sway of her arse. A horn blasted and brakes squealed. Someone shouted. The truck struck

Dave from the right, tossing him high. He landed on the footpath, his head cracked open and wet warmth pooling beneath the side of his face. He waited for the pain, for death, feeling strangely calm. The pool of blood spread, and with it the surge of his panic.

Mrs. Hennessy kneeled next to him, her hand on his shoulder. "You're all right. Everything's going to be okay." He tried to focus, but a thick liquid veil covered his eyes, blurring everything. The toddler wailed from his pram. "Stay with me," Mrs. Hennessy said. Dave's last thought before losing consciousness was that he had never imagined angels to have a flat, Midlands accent.

⁊⊗⊘

Dr. McCormack loomed over Dave in his hospital bed and listed his injuries in a singsong litany: fractured skull, smashed patella, three cracked ribs, and numerous hematomas. Dave could almost hear the rattle of his brokenness. He would have to undergo surgery on his right knee, the doctor continued, just as soon as the swelling on his brain came down. "All things considered, you're a very lucky man." Dave didn't know what horrified him more: the extent of his injuries or seeing his swaddled head twinned in the doctor's spectacles.

Day eight in the hospital, Dave lay recovering from a successful knee surgery. By then, the constant pain, noise, boredom, vital checks, and taint of antiseptic were overwhelming. He'd clicked the dispenser on his morphine drip so often a blister had formed on his thumb. The obsessive action was pointless, the drip's dose timed and regulated, but he couldn't stop himself. His attention returned to the orange plastic chair next to his bed, forever empty. He signaled to a nurse, the one with the wide parting in her hair like a scar. "Please take that away."

Dave was seven when his mother died from multiple sclerosis. The chairs by her hospital bed were gray. "We don't cry," his father said.

A bug-eyed orderly appeared with yet another dismal lunch on a brown plastic tray. Dave picked at the tough beef and dried potatoes and consoled himself with the tub of raspberry ripple ice cream. A squat nurse arrived to prod and poke. Just as she asked after his latest bowel movement, a second nurse approached, her face splattered with dark freckles. "You have a visitor."

Mrs. Hennessy slow-walked into the male ward, every eye trained on her top-heavy figure and those long legs inside fitted white jeans, a matching jacket folded over her crossed forearms. She removed a green, glossy apple from the jacket's pocket and held it out on her palm. Such a curious, childish thing to bring, and yet the offering sent the same rush through his veins as the morphine. He couldn't stop the smile that cracked his face. She placed the apple on his bedside locker and floated down onto the orange chair, brought back by the square-jawed orderly.

She whistled low. "McMurtagh's truck did a right job. Almost made sand and gravel out of you."

Every person in town and beyond knew McMurtagh's trucks, their convoys constantly on the go at speed, transferring loads from quarries to sites. She looked at his pillows rather than his face. He imagined what she'd seen at the accident—the blood from his head splattered on the concrete like a fired paintball bullet. He must still look repulsive. He pictured his puffy face, as pale in places as his bandages, and the rest a mess of bluish bruises and grazed, open skin. Even before the accident, he hadn't cut much of a figure. At fifty-five, he had a belly, gray in his brown hair, and his equally dull eyes were set too far apart beneath straight brows. At least he was tall and, usually, smooth-skinned.

"Did you just come here to praise the truck?" he said.

"I thought you might need help once you get out. That you might want to hire me? The babysitting's wrecking my head."

He chuckled as best his injuries would allow. Her expression hardened and she lifted her heart-shaped chin. "What's so funny?"

~ ❦ ~

On the day of Dave's discharge, Mrs. Hennessy arrived to the hospital an hour late, her blue-black curls looking freshly dyed and bouncing on her narrow shoulders. His relief at her showing up as promised turned to anger. "Where've you been?"

She ignored him and reached for the black marker on his food tray. With a flourish, she autographed the top of his leg cast, right at its neck. Fresh disappointment nipped. "Cora?" The name felt hard and wrong in his mouth. "Can I call you something else?"

She laughed, a single crack. "You're not very good with people, are you?"

The taxi arrived at Dave's, an attached redbrick in an estate of identical houses on the edge of town. Cora pulled him up and out of the front seat and dropped him into his wheelchair.

Arrows of pain shot down his injured leg and up into his lower back. "Take it easy, can't you."

"I'm not superwoman, you have to help me," she said.

He wheeled his chair around her and propelled himself along his front path, temper giving him strength. His next-door neighbor, Tom, appeared out of his house. Tom was a sixtyish, gray-haired widower whose various children came and went on weekends and special occasions. Dave had phoned him from the hospital, the brief exchange the most they'd spoken to each other in nearly ten years of living side by side. Dave didn't like to get too close to his neighbors, or anyone else. "Less people, less to mend," his father used to say.

Tom and the taxi driver backed Dave and his wheelchair up the eight front steps. Each thump reminded Dave of the smash of the truck.

"Home sweet home," Tom said at the open front door.

"That'll do," Dave said and wheeled inside.

⟨✦⟩

"Where should I put these?" Cora held up Dave's *Get Well* cards, one from the Road Safety Department and the others from the students and teachers at St. Brendan's School. He almost told her to throw them away—he didn't recognize most of the scribbled names—but thought twice and pointed to the mantelpiece.

While Cora made up his rented hospital bed inside the living room, Dave sipped a sweaty can of ale and watched an old film from his collection of classic videos, *Night Gallery* with Joan Crawford. He caught Cora in his peripheral vision, reaching over the plastic-covered mattress, struggling to fix the bottom sheet. A large tattoo spanned her lower back, the wings of a hawk, or maybe an eagle. The ink was dark, a recent acquisition. He snorted to himself. She was a bit big in the ears for getting fresh ink. She straightened and met his eyes. His attention jumped back to the TV and Joan Crawford's sightless, chilling stare.

That evening, as Cora prepared to leave, he rolled past her and held the front door open.

"So you can be a gentleman, good to know," she said, smirking. He smiled, almost forgetting his injuries.

⟨✦⟩

The next morning, Dave wheeled to his living room window. Smog shadowed the street, like something lurking. Several minutes expired with only the birds, cars, passersby, and Tom's cocoa-colored Labrador for company. The dog lay stretched out on his back in

Tom's front garden, his pale belly turned to the sky like an insect in trouble.

The row of redbrick homes across the street looked dirty and dull, crumbling. Straight opposite, in the house rented to college students, the gray net curtains clung to the windows, as if glued to the glass by grime. From the TV, news of rising unemployment, immigration, homelessness, and gangland wars. Cora appeared on the street and Dave's chest went up like a matchstick meeting sulfur. His excitement cooled. There was a lad walking alongside her. Clad all in black, the twenty-something worked a swagger and a buzz cut.

Dave answered his front door, a hurling stick lying across the arms of his wheelchair. Cora eyed the hurley with a mix of amusement and contempt.

"Who's he?" Dave asked.

"He's scared of me." The lad's glee made his voice high, like a boy's on the verge of changing.

Cora ran her tongue over her top lip, her eyes laughing. "Relax. This is my fella, Kieran. I thought it best to bring him along. I'm never going to manage you and those front steps on my own."

"Your fella?" Dave said, confused. Maybe they were mother and son. The lad was young enough. But they couldn't look more different. His brown scalp fuzz paled next to Cora's raven locks, and his mouth looked dark and malnourished next to her thick, fruity lips. As if to right the record, Kieran draped his arm around Cora's shoulders and rubbed her earlobe between his thick fingers. The odd intimacy made Dave feel a little sick. "I don't need his help."

"Well I do, okay? Now come on, we need to do a shop, you've nothing but tins and frozen," Cora said.

Outside the Spar, Cora pulled Dave's Toyota into a handicap space. Dave hadn't yet received his disabled parking tag and worried he'd get a ticket.

"Kieran can stay in the car and move it if needs be," she said.

"Steal it more like." Dave still had an uneasy feeling, like they were playing him.

Kieran piped up from the back seat. "If I was going to steal a car I'd pick a decent one."

While Cora wheeled Dave away, the lad revved the engine hard, a grin stitched across his face. Dave's head throbbed with temper.

Inside the supermarket, Cora asked him his wants and needs. As they moved up and down the aisles, Dave caught himself pretending they lived together, a couple. He pressed his cracked ribs, reminding himself how it felt when things went bad.

At last he and Cora exited the Spar, bags of shopping hanging from her wrists and several more sitting on his lap. "You took your time," Kieran said, sliding out from behind the driver's seat and helping Cora load the bags. He lifted Dave out of his chair and into the front passenger seat. Dave gritted his teeth against the indignity.

Seated, he wiped himself down after Kieran's manhandling. "I'm not paying him a penny."

The dirty-white bubble of gum exploded on Cora's face. She chewed its splattered remains off her plump lips, a taunt in her eyes. "Keep up, can't you. It's only been euro and cent for how long now?"

"Just drive," Dave said.

She turned the key in the ignition and made that aggravated *phish* sound through her teeth. "Were you always like this or did McMurtagh's truck damage your personality as well?"

"Nice," Kieran said, laughing. Cora smiled at him in the rear-view, love in every tooth.

Cora arrived every morning around nine and stayed until evening. Dave had hired a handyman to build a wooden ramp out front, allowing him to glide down his front steps, but it remained a challenge for Cora to help push him back up the temporary fixture. They managed, though. Anything so he didn't have to suffer Kieran again.

Cora mostly cleaned, shopped, and prepared his meals. She introduced Dave to flavors and dishes he hadn't known existed. Just the thought of her spicy Hungarian goulash made him salivate. He hadn't dated in years, and even then he'd always avoided the homely type. Now he'd two women tending to him. Social welfare sent home help for an hour several times a week, to check in and give him a bed bath. Mary was big-boned and broad-faced, with dark facial hair and a motor mouth. She washed and witnessed his naked self, and they never looked at each other straight.

Despite his reticence, meal times with Cora became Dave's favorite part of the day. They would linger together at the table, eating, talking, and drinking cold, sweet white wine out of a box. One evening, Cora mentioned her sister. Liz was two years older and had immigrated to New Zealand more than twenty years ago. She rarely returned. "It's too expensive, and too far. But someday I'm going to go see her." She looked into the distance. "You need money to enjoy life properly, don't you? I don't care what anyone says, we're nothing without it."

His thoughts jumped to his settlement case. His solicitor reckoned he'd get six figures, more money than he knew what to do with.

"What about you? Any family?" she asked.

His dad died twelve years ago, and he and his older brother hadn't had contact in nearly a decade. "We dropped out of each other's lives."

"I'm sorry," she said.

They locked eyes. Just as he was working up to say something about how nice it was to have her around, she jumped from her chair and reached into the cabinet. Her shirt rode up, flashing the tattoo on her back.

"Is it a hawk?" he asked.

"A crow."

"Oh." He felt the same disappointment as when she'd written her name on his cast.

She laughed. "Why don't people like crows? They're fierce and intelligent, totally misunderstood."

He almost said crows were a bad omen but her open face and shiny eyes stopped him.

꩜

Another late afternoon, Dave scanned the *Indo* at the kitchen table, pausing at the photograph of a group of Donegal secondary students, runners-up in an international science competition. To his surprise he suffered a pang, thinking of all those times he'd led a flock of dark, uniformed schoolchildren over the crosswalk, his stop sign raised high. Maybe the job was more than he'd believed it to be. Maybe, like carpentry, it was a kind of shaping and making. He pictured the teems of students trailing him, coached in the safe cross code and the importance of not going it alone.

He closed the newspaper, noticing for no good reason the date on the front page. His body was knitting itself back together and he would soon be free of his wheelchair, Cora's services no longer required.

A lie bubbled up. "What do you know? Today's my birthday."

Cora laughed. "You only realized that now?"

"I'm only seeing the date on the paper now. Come on—leave all that and we'll go out for something to eat, someplace nice."

She untied the strings of her apron in record time, its front stained orange from the carrots she'd skinned, and rushed into her jacket.

Dave, high on his deception and the promised settlement money, insisted on taking her to the Compass Grill, one of the fanciest restaurants in town. Cora protested. She was wearing jeans and a T-shirt. He directed her to the quays and its fashion boutiques, his treat. Elated, she didn't take the time to park properly, abandoning the car at an awkward angle and a good foot from the curb.

Inside the shop, she searched the racks with a shaky urgency, making the hangers screech. The saleswoman scowled, but Dave delighted in Cora's excitement. She wanted to try on black satin trousers and a gold top. He wanted her to purchase a dress. She gripped the arms of his wheelchair, her breath smelling of oatmeal. He could see down the front of her blouse, to her baby pink bra.

"I don't need another dress, Lollipop Man."

He'd always hated that title. At least traffic warden sounded somewhat respectable. But hearing it from her mouth made him flush with pleasure. He agreed to allow her buy whatever trousers and top she liked, but he wanted her to wear a dress to the restaurant. Her sticky, pink-infused lips brushed his cheek in thanks, making his skin hum.

She moved in and out of the dressing room, stunning in everything. Whenever she was out of view, Dave touched his fingers to his face and the memory of her kiss. Even after he'd decided on the red dress, he insisted she try on all the others. To every outfit, he silently assigned a different event and location, imagining them out on the town together, living the life.

Cora's three purchases decided on, she stood divine in the scarlet dress, her hair now gathered in a slick, dark bun. "You're a vision," he said. She laughed, blushing. The sales total came to almost five hundred euro. Dave didn't care. He pointed to the shiniest necklace inside the glass display, a cubic zirconia solitaire on a gold chain.

"It's too much, and it's your birthday, not mine," Cora said.

He purchased the necklace, seeing a flash of Cora and him flying to New Zealand, to visit her sister. She bent low in front of his wheel-chair and he fastened the chain at the back of her neck, his fingertips lingering on her bare skin.

⟨⊗⟩

At the restaurant, the champagne fizz danced on Cora's face. She laughed, revealing silver-filled molars. Dave raised his glass, also laughing as the tiny bubbles showered his nose and cheeks.

After the main course, lobster for Dave and filet mignon for Cora, the waiter brought them a large slice of chocolate cake topped with a lone blue candle on fire. Dave closed his eyes, wished for many more dates with Cora, and pushed his breath toward the flame. Cora clapped and he sat beaming. Gray smoke curled from the extinguished candle. He remembered, his smile collapsing. This was a lie.

The meal over and the champagne finished, he didn't want to go home. They decided on more drinks. Cora wheeled him into the Riverside Bar, with its view of the Shannon and the bright splashes of boats docked in the harbor. She made him feel like he was out on that river, the rock of the current unsteadying, and at the same time thrilling.

After two gin and tonics, Dave suspected his eyes looked as glazed as Cora's. She wagged her finger playfully. "You're a dark one. Full of surprises."

"I have more."

"Oh, yeah?"

He licked his lips and summoned his breath, just as he had be-fore blowing out his fake birthday candle. Trembling, he admitted, "After the accident, when you were leaning over me, I thought you were an angel." She laughed, her head tipped back. Embarrassed, he rushed to make light of his confession. "An angel with a flat, awful accent."

They stopped laughing. Her necklace sparkled under the lights, as if promising something. He rushed into the pause. "When I was a boy, I lost something. Something that was a huge deal."

Cora's face creased, her attention on him never so keen. "What was it?"

"Let's say it was a train set, vintage, spectacular—"

"A train set?"

"The point is, I think people, when they lose something they care that much about, they either keep chasing it, or they run in the opposite direction."

"You ran," she said, seeming far away. "And I chased."

He touched her, to bring her back. The barest flutter of his fat fingers at the wisp of dark hair feathering her cheekbone. "Maybe I've changed. Maybe I could chase, too."

Something in her eyes went out. "We should get going. I'll phone Kieran to come help us."

Anger flooded Dave with the same cold rush as the saline IV in the hospital. "I don't want that lad anywhere near us."

"We've had too much to drink. I can't get you home without him."

"What's the hurry? Aren't we having a grand time?" He touched his fingertips to her knee.

She moved her leg. His hand dropped through nothing. "I'm phoning Kieran."

"You can't be serious about him. You're old enough to be his mother—"

She stood up, her eyes smoldering. "This was a mistake."

He tugged on her wrist, pulling her back down. "Fine. Phone Kieran."

Kieran got drunk right off and stared goat-eyed at Cora. He winked at Dave. "She looks fierce hot in that red dress, doesn't she?"

Dave's thumb twitched, wanting to press the memory of the morphine drip.

Cora leaned toward him, flashing the tops of her breasts and holding him hostage. "Is he right? Do I look on fire?"

Kieran bounced around his chair, guffawing. Her performance was for him and not Dave. "Take me home. I've had enough of this."

"Oh so now you're ready?" she said.

The three moved out onto the street, Dave as rigid as his wheelchair with rage. Cora, laughing, staggering, couldn't get him into the car. Kieran, falling over himself with alcohol and laughter, reemerged from the back seat and helped as best he could. As the world spun, Dave tried to protest. Cora was too drunk to drive. They should take a taxi. But they were already out on the road, barreling over the tarmac.

By the time they arrived home, Dave felt violently ill. All that gin wasn't sitting well with the painkillers, champagne, and rich food. As soon as Kieran dragged him and his chair inside, Dave sped to the bathroom. He barely reached the toilet bowl in time. While he retched and spewed, Cora and the lad staggered down his hall. Dave vomited again.

Finished, Dave rolled to the kitchen and stopped short in the doorway. Kieran stood pressed against Cora, the two locked in an embrace of arms and tongues. Dave charged at them. "Get out, both of you."

He expected them to put up a fight, but they slipped past him, tripping and snickering like two schoolchildren caught drinking. He followed them up the hall. "And don't come back."

Cora turned to him, glassy-eyed, unsteady. "You need me."

"No, I don't." He rolled his chair forward, herding her and Kieran out the front door.

She stopped on the front step, a mix of pity and scorn shriveling her face. "It's not my fault you got notions."

"Wait, did he try something?" Kieran said, swaying, slurring.

Dave scoffed. "I got notions? Look at you two, it's disgusting."

"At least I have someone," she said.

The smack of McMurtagh's truck had hurt less.

Dave watched through the living room window, seeing Cora and Kieran disappear. Tom pulled up in his white Fiat. He and the Lab exited the car and moved up their front path. Dave waved and called out in greeting, the house accustomed now to the sound of voices.

# BEFORE STORMS HAD NAMES

FROM THE HILL, Rory Deavitt spotted the Morris Minor parked in the yard, the car hunter green and with a large black suitcase tied to its top. Whenever Mrs. Gillespie's guesthouse filled, she sometimes referred lodgers. Rory mostly welcomed the break from the everyday these infrequent visitors brought, with the exception of the mouthy Americans and the deadened married couples like his parents. He hoped this lodger might be someone closer to his age, and visiting from somewhere far beyond Ballinshere. Curious, expectant, he cleared the distance between the fields and farmhouse in minutes, not stopping to wash at the water pump.

He hesitated at the back door, hearing a rare excitement in Father's voice. The visitor responded in a soft, musical tone, thanking Rory's parents for agreeing to put her up—her accent Dublin, posh. Father laughed too hard. Perhaps he'd opened a bottle of Powers for the guest. Someone special so. Rory scraped the muck from his Wellingtons against the steel doormat and entered the kitchen, stopping at the edge of the room. There, at their scarred table sat the most striking woman he'd ever encountered in reality. She looked to be in her mid-thirties, with long black hair and a creamy, soft-boned face. Mother sat opposite, her rust-red hair flat and greasy. The woman quieted mid-sentence. Smiled at him. He spluttered a half-intelligible greeting.

"Don't just stand there, Rory, fetch Mrs. Moore's things from her car," Mother said.

"Please, call me Ashling."

Rory hauled the third and largest suitcase upstairs, conscious of Ashling climbing the steps behind him. Huffing, sweating, he couldn't hide how much he was struggling. He stepped up onto the landing, almost falling under the case's weight. His face blazed.

She trailed him into the guest bedroom and moved to the window. "What a view, it's beautiful."

"You think?" What was there to admire in shite-filled pastures and dumb, plodding cattle? In vast land cut with long, grasping shadows?

She glanced at him quizzically and returned her attention to the farm. Alone with her in the small bedroom, he felt especially self-conscious—his pimples whiter, his cow's lick taller, and his big toe peeking through his threadbare sock, the nail yellowed. Worse, he smelled of hay, sweat, cigarettes, and cow-shite. If she asked, he'd say he was eighteen.

"Thanks for your help," she said, already unpacking.

She removed a pine chess case finished in shiny lacquer and held together with bright brass hinges. She looked twice, seeming surprised to find him still there. "Do you play?"

He swallowed the impulse to mention his skill at draughts and shook his head.

"I can teach you while I'm here."

"You must be planning on staying a while so."

"I'm not in any hurry anywhere." She unlatched the chess case, revealing an assortment of pieces sculpted from blond and black woods. She'd carved them herself, she explained, from ancient bog oak. She handed him several pieces to examine. The top of the King's crown recalled a beggar's cupped hand. The knight's horse even had teeth, a series of tiny notches. Rory fought the urge to pocket it.

"You really should learn. It's a fascinating game."

He held the knight a moment longer in his large, dirty hand before dropping it onto the patchwork bedspread.

"No? What interests you then?"

His frustration surged. He couldn't summon the words and subject matters necessary to impress a woman like her, with her fancy accent and intelligent eyes the color of starlings' eggs. He hadn't had much learning. His parents had pulled him from school two years earlier, so he could work the farm full-time, lands and holdings in the Deavitt name for generations, despite the English, famine, emigration, and the worst of the worst of recessions. Father went so far as to claim that if you listened hard enough you could hear ancient Deavitt blood and bones stir beneath the soil.

"Something must call to you?"

"I dunno, really. I'm not one for making things, that's for sure."

She picked up a blond pawn. "I don't think of myself as making them, really. It's more like when I sculpt, I'm letting out whatever is already inside the lump of wood."

He felt the blood leave his face. Something inside him had long raged to get out, the adventurer, the would-be world traveler, but he was forever tied to this farmhouse and land, destined to keep it in the Deavitt name.

"Are you all right?"

"Fine."

She resumed unpacking. The silence stretched and his nerves got the better of him. At the doorway he reminded her that Mother would have dinner ready shortly. "She's not one to be kept waiting."

In the shower, Rory raked his fingernails over his body, digging into his armpits, groin, and the crack of his arse. No matter how hard he scrubbed, there was always that taint of livestock. After, he dressed in his favorite jeans and shirt, and hurried downstairs.

From her chair at the kitchen table, Mother looked him over, her lips pushed into a sour nub. Ashling appeared in the doorway. Mother's expression scarcely softened.

Father said grace, his ruddy hands clasped, his broken fingernails dark with dirt. The smell of meat, mint, and rosemary hung over the kitchen, as oppressive as the leftover heat from the oven.

Mother carved the leg of lamb, sweat bubbling on the fuzz over her lips. "So you're from Dublin, Mrs. Moore?"

"Yes, a city girl." She gave a small laugh. "I hope you won't hold it against me."

"And you're travelling alone?"

Rory followed Mother's pointed gaze to the band of pale skin circling the bottom of Ashling's ring finger.

"You've such a beautiful home," Ashling said.

"And yours is where, did you say?"

Rory looked to Father, hoping he'd put a stop to Mother's inquisition, but the man appeared oblivious, shoveling gravied meat and potato into his wet mouth.

"Nowhere's home at the moment," Ashling said.

"I see," Mother said.

Father paused the annihilation of his dinner, his once broad shoulders reduced to downward slopes. "I'd say you get great mileage from that Morris Minor? Had one myself years back. Even had a name for her."

"No one wants to hear your foolishness," Mother said.

"Lucy," Father said. "As in Lucille Ball. Great little car, never gave me a moment's bother."

"Oh, please," Mother said. "It wasn't fit to house chickens in the end."

"There was plenty of life left in her," Father said.

"It was going, or I was," Mother said.

"How could I forget," Father said.

Ashling watched Rory with those large, wide-set eyes. He couldn't decide if he liked or hated her sympathy.

⁘

As soon as dinner finished, Ashling excused herself from the kitchen. Father remained at the table, working a sliver of carrot between his teeth with a broken matchstick. Mother curled a wad of bread and sopped up the last of the lamb juices from her plate. "She's a strange one."

Rory stood up, hands curled tight. "It's beyond me why anyone would pay to stay here and put up with you and your prying."

"Are you going to let him talk to me like that?" Mother said.

"Don't talk to your mother like that," Father said.

While his parents snipped and gossiped, Rory washed the dishes with fervor, smacking the water and scrubbing the stains. His parents fell silent.

"Rory? How about that lesson?" Ashling asked, the chess case hanging from her hand.

"Chess, is it?" Father said, his voice again hitting those high notes from earlier. "I used to play years ago." His delight climbed. "And look at this beauty." He opened the lacquered case on the table and gushed at the carved pieces. "Are you seeing this, Dolores? Aren't they something?"

"Tedious game," Mother said, barely glancing over.

"Let's play, shall we?" Father rushed from the kitchen to the living room, the chess case under his arm.

"All right then," Ashling said, laughing. She smiled apologetically at Rory and followed.

⌘

The next morning, Rory lingered in bed before daybreak, fantasizing about Ashling in the room next to his, no more than ten hands length away. He tested her name in a whisper, liking the soft start of it and the little flick of his tongue at the end. It meant 'dream' if he remembered his Irish well enough. He imagined speaking it into her soft neck as he stretched himself over her.

⌘

After milking the cows and returning the herd to the pasture, Rory and Father worked the hayfields through the morning and into the vengeful noonday sun. Early afternoon, the much-awaited silhouette shimmered in the distance—Mother arriving with their lunch.

Only it wasn't.

"If it isn't herself!" Father rushed to free Ashling of the picnic basket hanging from the crook of her arm. "I hope you're not vexed with me after last night?"

"Never. All's fair in love and chess."

Rory grabbed an egg salad sandwich from the basket and ate furiously. Why couldn't the old fool go off someplace and leave them alone? Did he not realize how daft he sounded, clueless that she'd surely let him win? Ashling settled on the baked ground and leaned against the haystack between father and son, her shoulder brushing Rory's and setting off sparks beneath his skin.

"Are you up for another game this evening?" Father asked, a doting grin on his face. "I promise to go easy on you this time."

"I believe Rory wants his turn at besting me tonight," she said.

"I doubt he even knows how to play. Do you, son?"

"You've no idea what I know."

"I envy you both living here," Ashling said.

Again with her praise of these endless fields, and the sycamores like sentries. She reached into the picnic basket and removed a short knife and small piece of bog oak. She resumed carving what looked like a doll with surprising life in its face.

When Father said as much, Ashling laughed kindly. "Actually, it's a mermaid." She went on to explain her process, how the rough cuts gave way to finer details, then the several rounds of sanding, and for the finish, a few coats of linseed oil.

Father studied the mermaid-in-making. "Wasn't it Van Dyke who wrote a book about a mermaid?"

"It was Hans Christian Andersen, you ape." At least Rory had stayed in school long enough to know that much.

"I was close," Father said, the warmth in his eyes trained on Ashling.

After a time, she returned her knife and mermaid to the basket. She stood up and dusted the hay and dirt from the back of her faded jeans. "I think I'll take a walk down as far as the river." She pointed to the woods. "Straight through there, right?"

Rory jumped to his feet. "I'll show you."

"You're not going anywhere," Father said, pitchfork in-hand. "We've a day's work to do yet. She'll manage fine on her own, won't you, dear?" Again with that boyish smile, the shine in his eyes.

The men returned home that evening to find a maroon Hillman Avenger parked in the yard. Rory's stomach turned to lead. If this were another lodger, he'd have to give up his bedroom and sleep on the living room couch.

Peter, tall and gangly, appeared down to dinner dressed in brown cords and loafers, his salmon-colored shirt buttoned low, revealing dark chest hair like wild, wiry creatures. From Ashling's glances, she didn't seem to mind his taste in clothes, or his menagerie.

As hard as Rory tried, it proved impossible not to like Peter. A Belfast man, he had a contagious grin and playful manner, even if he did seem confident that his every word would meet with only favor. He engaged Rory in conversation like an equal, talking about football, Gaelic and soccer, and the ongoing stalemate between Thatcher and the hunger strikers.

"Iron Bitch," Rory said.

Mother dispatched a laugh, her hand patting curls still smelling of hairspray from the salon. She'd also painted her face with rare makeup, bringing out the tea in her eyes and hay in her hair. Her royal-blue blouse looked fresh from the dry cleaners. "You'll have to forgive my son, Peter, he's trying to sound big in front of you."

"He's not wrong." Peter's side-eye asked Rory *How can you suffer it?* He addressed Ashling, leaving Rory cringing. "So you're a sculptor. I did woodwork in school and am only sorry I didn't keep at it."

"It's not too late," Ashling said. "Our art never leaves us."

"Maybe you could give me a refresher course?"

"I'm sure we could track down some bog wood around here," Ashling said, blushing, smiling. "That is if you don't mind, Mr. Deavitt?"

"Not at all," Father said, his voice dull.

"It's settled then," Peter said. "Let's go."

"What? Now?" Ashling said laughing.

"You can't go anywhere," Mother said. "The dinner's not finished, and I made my Bakewell tart specially."

"Yes, stay," Father said, an equally embarrassing plea in his voice.

"This was lovely, really, thank you." Peter stood up. Ashling, too.

Rory watched them leave with a feeling like sleep paralysis, where you can't move, can't cry out for help.

⚶

By the time Ashling and Peter returned, Rory's parents had long retired to bed. If the lodgers noticed Rory lying on the couch, they didn't let on, but continued upstairs, shushing and giggling. Rory pictured them drinking whiskey at one of the corner tables for two inside Flaherty's, knowing that they would favor jiggers of amber and fire over weaker fare.

The upstairs landing creaked and Ashling's bedroom door eased open. Hot whispers followed, and the door clicked closed. Rory stayed as long as he could bear it on the couch before struggling from the tangle of blankets.

He paused outside the guest bedroom, his head as close to the door as he dared. The bed frame squeaked. Muffled panting and gasping followed, punctuated by moans. He remained in the hall, the floorboards having turned to water beneath him.

The bedroom door pulled open and Peter filled the doorway. Rory stared past him to Ashling lying naked on the bed, her black hair fanning the pillows just as in his fantasies. This was his first time to see a naked woman in the flesh. Her breasts appeared smaller than he'd pictured and her dark nipples glared. The muff of black hair between her legs seemed impossibly dark and dense.

Peter pulled the door closed behind him and stood too close. "Go back to bed, son."

Rory returned to the couch, and pulled at himself until he felt raw.

⚶

Rory awoke in the early hours to the sound of Mother shouting in the kitchen, a rant about sin. Father, the tired voice of reason, tried to calm her. After several rapid-fire rounds, he climbed the stairs with a heavy tread.

Peter's outraged laughter carried through the house. He clattered down the stairs. Mother met him in the hall. Rory felt soldered to the couch.

"You should be ashamed of yourself, you and that hussy," Mother said.

"More like well satisfied," Peter said. His car tore out of the yard with a grinding churn.

Rory plodded into the kitchen, still in his striped pajamas. Mother startled, her wet eyes ringed in red. "That Peter," she spat. "You're not to turn into a dirty article like him, do you hear me?"

꘡꘡꘡

Ashling entered the kitchen to take breakfast, her expression stormy. Mother didn't hesitate. "I'm sure you understand, Mrs. Moore, why we sent Peter packing. This is a God-fearing house and there'll be no more of the goings-on we had to endure last night. Is that clear?"

Ashling looked down at her plate, her hands locked under her chin. "I'm a grown woman and a paying customer, Mrs. Deavitt, and I'd like to eat my breakfast in peace."

"Not before I add, Mrs. Moore, that I find those naked sculptures in your bedroom offensive. I'll thank you to put them away."

"Now, Dolores," Father said. "That's none of our business." He addressed Ashling. "How's the mermaid coming along?"

She smiled gratefully. "Well, thank you, it's almost finished."

"Does this sea creature also have her tits bared?" Mother said.

Rory lifted his foot beneath the table and kicked Mother hard on the shin. She roared and bucked in her chair. He rushed out the back door. Father shouted, demanding he return.

✌∽

Rory arrived at the river, out of breath. He could still hear Mother's cry, see her shock and pain. He dropped to sitting on the riverbank. Fuck her, and Father. He grabbed at pebbles and dirt and fired them into the moving river. Any mention from him of any ambition other than the farm had only ever infuriated Father and elicited scorn from Mother.

"What else would you do?" Father said.

"Where else would have you?" Mother said.

Something moved behind him. Relief and delight flooded his head. Ashling had followed him, just as he'd hoped. She drifted onto the grass beside him and smoothed her skirt over her knees. She smelled sweet and foreign. Of coconut, he realized.

"I'm leaving," she said. "I think that's best."

He fired larger pebbles and deeper, darker dirt at the river, an insistent throb annoying his chest, as if his heart was kicking him.

"You're not much of a talker, are you? The dark, brooding type." Her shoulder nudged his playfully, delivering the same pain-pleasure charge as the electric fences in the far field, to keep the cattle in check.

She struggled to her feet and moved to the river's edge. She squatted on her hunkers, her long dark hair like a mantle on her back, and dipped her finger into the water. He recalled the mermaid, her etched hair fanning her narrow back and the crown of tiny sculpted flowers surrounding her head.

"What happened to your husband?"

She looked up but kept her back to him. "I left him."

"Why?"

Her finger resumed its lazy travel through the water. "There was no good reason left to stay."

The tightness in his chest worsened, like giant hands clenching his lungs. She pulled her finger from the river and smiled up at him. "I drew something, see?"

He looked at the water and shrugged.

"Come on. You're not even trying."

"Don't be stupid. There's nothing there." Wasn't she smart with her illusions? With how she made things out of nothing and nothing out of things. He scrambled to his feet and towered over her. He lifted a rock with both hands and raised it high. Hurled the missile. She drew back from the river's splash.

"You don't just up and leave. You can't walk away from your husband and home like they mean nothing—"

She stood up. "This was a mistake. I should go."

"Do that."

She started up the slope of the riverbank. He could also make something out of nothing. Could grab her waist from behind. Could pull her to the ground. Could make her take at least his spill from this place.

He dropped onto his back. Bounced his head against the earth, once, twice. Harder. He stared at the passage of ghostly clouds—their hidden, trapped figures at the mercy of the whip of the weather.

# BLUE HOT

HE SPILLED BLOOD on our first date. I'm inclined to say the gush from the nose of the youngfella he punched ran purple and pretty, but making poetry of that fight would be a lie. I lied about him for so long, to others, to myself, the habit still has teeth.

Our date was going great until the fight—dinner, drinks, and a late film in town. I was seventeen, he was eighteen, and his taking me out was this unbelievable wish-come-true. I can't remember what film we saw inside the Adelphi Cinema. Funny, that. After, we kissed in his dad's Ford on the street, our mouths wet and warm. The air freshener dangling from the rearview was strawberry scented and his aftershave sent up hints of citrus. Or probably that's more of my poet getting out.

Three youngfellas rapped on the car roof, jeering, snickering. "Stick your mickey in her mouth."

He pulled a crowbar from beneath the driver's seat and rushed from the car, letting the length of metal fly.

On the drive home, I couldn't stop shaking.

"Come on," he said. "That wasn't my fault. They came looking for it."

Back on New Year's Eve, I'd gone to the sports club disco looking for him. Over a hundred of us packed the large hall, revving up for midnight. The sagging Christmas decorations had hung from the club's ceiling and walls since early December, mostly blots of blue-white stars, streaks of silver and gold tinsel, and strings of multicolored fairy lights. I drank hard, vodka with coke, ice, and lemon. I also danced hard, the music, the alcohol, igniting my limbs. I laughed hard, too. Boys are attracted to girls who look like they're loads of fun, or who seem especially tragic. I'd read that in a glossy magazine. Or maybe I'd heard it on the radio, TV, or bus.

"Do you think he even knows I exist?" I asked my best friend.

"He's staring straight at you."

"Seriously? Oh God really?"

She dragged me onto the dance floor. "Let's give him a right good show."

I tracked him tracking me. When he watched me from the sidelines. When he went to the bar to down pints and jiggers. When he talked and laughed with the in crowd.

Those first beats of the slow dance set right before midnight, my racing heart seemed capable of grievous bodily harm. If he was going to ask me to dance, make any kind of move, it was now or never. When he walked toward me, my heart slammed into my ribcage.

While we danced, I rested my head on his shoulder, my arms around his neck locking us together and his arms around my waist a belt of electricity. At midnight we kissed for the first time, his lips cool, soft. It was the best kind of falling. After the disco, he invited me back to his gaff. My heart was a shooting star.

In the back room, while his parents and siblings slept overhead, we listened to Bob Dylan on the record player and lay together next to a gas heater, its fake fire burning orange and blue. No way in my house we could afford to burn the heater on high, and most certainly not for some fella and me.

He rubbed my breasts, slid his finger in and out, and lay on top of me. I pulled on him, and we almost went all the way, but I decided *no, let's wait*. I'd learned somewhere to keep a man hungry, eager. Because once satisfied he would move on to his next conquest. Men got to do that.

It was the farthest I'd ever gone. Technically. I'd only had one steady boyfriend before that night, and we never went further than kissing. That's all I'd ever volunteered, anyways. That other stuff was forced on me years back by a bloated, middle-aged neighbor who tasted of milk—sometimes sour, or even worse sweet.

Now, next to the gas fire and the circling record album, my dream catch rocked against my pubic bone like I was the music he was keeping time to. The heater the color of a peach sunset above blue mountains warmed my skin to hurting, but I didn't move or complain. I didn't dare break the spell.

✒⊗⦶

The night after our first date and the fight outside the cinema, he showed up at my front door, his apology and promises heartfelt. Tortured declarations bigger and better than anything I'd ever heard. Of course that wasn't setting the bar very high. But I could tell how sorry he was, and I knew nothing like that nightmare fight would ever happen again. Not even close.

No matter how hard I tried to wring those images from my head, they wouldn't fall away—the three lads warding off his blows with the crowbar by swinging their jackets through the night like shields; he and the biggest of them battering each other; and me getting between them, begging them to stop.

He and I saw each other every chance we could get.

My best friend said, "Hey, remember me?"

She was joking, although I did see her, all of my friends, less and less. His circle were the older crowd with cars and jobs, a few even in college, others engaged to be married or in the family way, and most with hero status in football, hurling, or break dancing. So much that was shiny and bright.

Speaking of. His brother's girlfriend was gorgeous. Golden hair, dreamy blue eyes, pale, dewy skin. I could only guess at the number of fellas who wanted to be her catwalk. Whenever we were together, in the pub, at football matches, or in various parks and houses, wherever, we'd be bubbling over inside because we were the Buckley brothers' girls. Kind and funny—and like me wrecked from all the aggro at home—I loved being around her and longed to catch some of her glow.

This one time, she parked her dad's car at the edge of the sports pitch and we watched our men play in yet another championship football match. We cheered and sneaked cold lager from tall, slippery cans, all four car windows rolled down to nothing.

Points were won and lost on the field. Goals scored and saved. Knees skinned, limbs bruised, heads knocked. Our team was winning and our men were playing gloriously. My insides wheeled with pleasure. This would all be driving him happy.

His brother's girlfriend and I downed the last of the six-pack and laughed ourselves empty. Then we were crying. Her ma. My ma. Blah. Blah. Blah. The final whistle blew, our team the victors.

"Shit," she said, hopping across the handbrake and landing next to me on the passenger seat. She pulled down the sun visor and wiped her damp face with both hands.

A cold feeling came over me, more my insides than my skin. "Can I see?" I set about fixing my own mascara-streaked face. We looked like two little girls in the glass, our faces shrunken and strangely frightened.

She took one last check, sniffling and turning her head. She pulled down the vee of her white T-shirt and lifted her yellow hair off her shoulders, shaking it out like the wings of a canary. "Do I look okay?"

"You look fabulous."

She flipped the sun visor back into place.

"Me?" I asked.

She smiled, her eyes calm now. "You're lovely."

I smiled back. She returned to the driver's seat. We sat up straight, looking out at our men walking toward the clubhouse and the showers. Their backs had to hurt, all those congratulatory slaps.

I should have felt delighted. The lads would be on a high. The craic tonight would be fierce. But I was still rattled. She'd seemed scared, and it had infected me. But what was there to be afraid of? We'd won.

***

His family, house, furniture, food, TV, crackling fire, even their dog was better than ours. His mother, warm, smiley, owned a florist and smelled of roses and jasmine. A fantastic cook, she made me feel full and worthy. I envied how he and her teased and laughed together, took care of each other.

"Did you get enough to eat? Are you warm enough? Don't forget you have an interview tomorrow," she'd say.

He made her cups of tea and asked about her day at the flower shop. Urged her to treat herself to a hairdo, an afternoon's shopping, or to get out and about with friends. "You deserve it."

"One of these days," she said, spooning our dessert into glazed bowls the color of the sea at its deepest blue.

My granny used to say that the way a man treats his mother is the way he will treat you. I had only turned eighteen but already I was dreaming about being his wife, and our curly-haired babies, and how well we'd look after each other.

I wasn't sure what to make of Mr. Buckley. He was pleasant enough, but it was hard not to notice how my man tensed whenever his dad was around. I'd feel his skeleton tighten and spot the pulse above his jaw jump as soon as Mr. Buckley entered the room. The time we skipped Mass on a holy day of obligation, his dad uttered a string of curses and slammed the living room door.

Mr. Buckley got home late a lot, too, closing the pub with the best of them. Once that I know of, he sported a black eye; another time, a burst lip.

"Is your dad okay?" I asked.

He delivered that sharp headshake that said *leave it*. When he spoke, he sounded exhausted. "He's fine."

I swallowed the urge to say more. Long before him, I'd learned when not to press a thing. My da avoided our house, and Ma, as much as possible, and didn't appreciate questions about his whereabouts. I snuggled closer, touching my forehead to the side of my man's neck, smelling the mingle of cigarettes and his spicy body odor. I could feel the heat and beat of him. I closed my eyes, recalling the gas heater from that first night he brought me here, the flickering oranges and blues, the biting blaze.

꧁◈꧂

My man loved that I was skinny with big tits, and preferred me in black clothes that fit like a second skin. Sometimes he liked that other fellas stared, but not always. Those times he squared up to lads and thumped a few heads. We got thrown out of places.

"You promised," I said.

"What the fuck?" he said. "You can't put that on me."

One time he said with feeling, "Wear your black mini dress on Friday night, the silky one with red stripes. I'll take you someplace nice." My skin erupted in tiny bumps. No one had ever made me feel so special. Desired. That perv neighbor who tasted of milk had claimed that's what he was doing, but I was scared and ashamed back then, not stupid.

Ma liked my boyfriend. He was polite and charming, and treated her with respect, as if she were the same as the other mothers. That helped keep the peace between her and me some. Other times, seeing me happy gave her temper claws.

In the lead-up to that Friday and his promise of someplace nice, my insides were humming with anticipation. Long before this we'd gone all the way together and not only had he not moved on to someone else, we were secretly paying off on a ruby engagement ring studded with a round of tiny diamonds that sent out bolts of light.

"What are you so happy about?" Ma said.

Later, on my bed, I found the few clothes I cherished cut to pieces.

I charged downstairs and into the kitchen, shreds of black and red silk spilling from my hand. "Where did you put the scissors? If I find those scissors."

But there was nothing of hers I could destroy in revenge. There wasn't anything she cared much about. Not anymore. Drunk, she took to screaming. Then she started crying. "Isn't it well for you."

✺

I pulled open our front door and his smile collapsed. He whirled around and marched down our path. "Hey," I said, following him, feeling panicked.

He swung around at our gate. "I told you to wear the silk dress."

"I know, I'm sorry—"

He charged across the road. I caught up with him at his car.

"You don't like this?" I asked, flirting. I performed a spin in my black satin shirt and blacker velvet pants.

"Get in the car."

He drove fast. So fast I started praying. He rammed the heel of his hand into the steering wheel. "I swear I'll drive us into a wall." His voice rose. "Is that what you want? You want me to drive us into a wall?"

"No. Stop it. Calm down, would you?"

"Why won't you do what you're told? I said I'd something special planned."

My chest hurt, as if my blood was pumping into the wrong places. "Ma destroyed it, okay? She took a scissors to it and cut it up."

His eyes jumped from the road to me, his forehead a row of divots. "Why would she do that?"

"Cause she's crazy. You know she's crazy."

He slowed the car and studied me. Then reached for my shoulder, squeezing my bones. "It's okay. I get it now. You should have told me."

I wanted to bawl, but managed not to. I almost said sorry again, but stemmed that as well. That whole night, I thought of the other things I wanted to make stop.

✺❀✺

For weeks he remained on his best behavior and I allowed myself to believe.

"I'm glad you two are figuring it out," his brother's now fiancé said, pressing her yellow hair to her neck. She laughed, its undercurrent faulty. "Just think, we could both be Mrs. Buckleys." I pictured my promised engagement ring locked inside the dark, closed jewelers in town, sunk into that slot in its black velvet box, waiting to wear me.

Another night, another time he and I were drunk, he kicked over a chair in my living room and lashed his denim jacket across my head. Saturday, at a friend's house party, he swore it never happened, but I could still feel the sting of those metal buttons. I kept goading him, needing to see how far he would go—hoping, convincing myself, that he would never hurt me any worse than he already had.

There in the dark garden, he bunched my hair in his fist, threatening to smash my head against the concrete wall. "Do it," I said through gritted teeth.

He yanked my head backward, making me cry out and sending that New Year's Eve night into reverse, undoing its every frame. He didn't take me to his house after the disco. Didn't kiss me at midnight. Didn't ask me to dance. The more he shook me, the more he erased us, until I'd never gone looking for it from him in the first place, that thing called love.

# WILDE

INSIDE THE DUBLIN GUESTHOUSE, over a breakfast of peppery scrambled eggs, I sat watching the young couple below on the street. They stood on the opposite side of the road, next to the bus stop's thin yellow pole, bundled up in woolen accessories and thick, dark jackets. They pressed their bodies together, their arms clasping each other's waist, and rocked from side to side for warmth, their breaths smoke. They put me in mind of Da and his imaginary friend, Mary, waltzing around our kitchen together.

I was alone inside the dining room on Northumberland Road, still jetlagged on day two of my annual trip back home. Beyond the second-floor window, the gray-black February morning lightened, the sky soon looking wiped clean. The long line of traffic with grasping headlights rolled forward. A giant, naked tree stretched across my bird's-eye view, its branches sprawling. Like the couple at the bus stop, the tree swayed in constant motion. The wind picked up, battering everything.

I set out from the guesthouse, disappointed the air had stilled. There's nothing like great gusts, how they blast, clear. At the gate, I turned right. The previous night, I'd turned left on the blackened street and left again onto Haddington Road, discovering shops, pubs, restaurants, and a lone laundrette. This right turn would take me over the Grand Canal and should lead straight to Grafton Street, if I remembered rightly. I hesitated, second-guessing myself. I was raised on the Northside, far from this exclusive neighborhood. I pressed ahead over the canal, deciding to explore. The chill morning was bitter but dry, and I had nowhere I needed to be. I could risk getting lost.

I soon passed Merrion Square Park and stood marveling through its green railings at the life-size statue of Oscar Wilde. He lay reclining provocatively on a large granite boulder, the bronze monument surrounded by tourists and students, their phones and cameras aimed. The memorial tugged. Up close, Wilde's black trousers glittered and the collar and cuffs of his green jacket bloomed pink. Now his was a name. Nothing like Mary, as plain as milk. Wilde stared down, managing to look both smug and glum. The blackened flower in his hand made me think of his fairy tale, "The Happy Prince." Perhaps the colorless carnation, like the prince, had sacrificed its beauty to benefit others.

I touched Wilde's right shoe and let my hand rest on its gleam. A streaky rasher of a man ordered me to step aside so he could snap photos. I remained, claiming my time, and at my leisure moved to the two stone pillars opposite. A bronze sculpture crowned each one, the first of Wilde's pregnant wife, Constance, and the second the torso of the Greek god Dionysus. Wilde's quotes, written in gold ink, adorned the base of the pillars. I told myself that the first quote my eyes landed on would be a signpost. I was ready for a new life chapter—had been ever since my divorce four years earlier. The ache, the restlessness, had turned manic now that my third son was headed for college in August, leaving me alone in our three-bedroom brownstone in Chicago's South Side, the last house in the cul-de-sac. I read the first Wilde quote my eyes found, a quip about breakfast that offered me nothing.

*✺*

Along Clare Street, in the window of a brightly lit art gallery, a black-and-white photograph of Seamus Heaney also pulled. Heaney, wearing silver-rimmed glasses and a dark Aran jumper, sat reading a book, its title blurred. I recalled his poem about peeling potatoes with his mother, less the lines themselves and more how they made me feel. Of all his work that I'd read, that domestic poem pressed.

Da's ravings and Mary's arrival had alarmed my family—I could never forget that shivery eeriness on first seeing through the hallucinatory eyes of a madman—but we soon came to accept, even embrace, Mary's presence. Her appearance cracked open Da's years-long depression, an abyss we'd lost hope of anyone, anything, ever penetrating.

A man spoke up next to me, his voice flamboyant, commanding. "I declare dripping, not dipping, the superior word."

"Sorry?" I said, turning my head. I felt only a moment's startlement, and then a knowing calm. Clearly, the theme of the day was conjuring, and if I was going to call forth anyone, why not the great Oscar Wilde. No bland Marys for me, thanks very much.

"The knives," Oscar said impatiently.

I silently recited the line in question from Heaney's poem twice, testing both words. "Either works," I said. But 'dipping knives' was undoubtedly the better choice.

"Well don't dally," Wilde said, moving off in the direction of his alma mater.

*✺*

Inside Hodges Figgis, Wilde located his books. I traced a red-brown spine with reverence, my finger pausing on *Portrait*. "What's that like, after all this time?"

"I expected nothing less," he said.

Inside Carluccio's, he drank espresso and spoke fluent Italian, his eyes darting to everyone but me. Mary had served Da so much better, in the beginning at least. The whole scene put me in mind of my marriage—how Ben and I had taken each other for granted all those years. How invisible we became to one another.

Wilde scribbled on a paper napkin. He was sizable, flabbing. Just as with Ben, I couldn't decide what stopped him from being all-out handsome. The hooded eyes, I posited. His hawkish air. It certainly wasn't his flagrant lips. He demanded more napkins. So many napkins, a white wall of words rose between us.

He wrote through three pens, until his right hand cramped, and next his left. I hadn't known he was ambidextrous. Then he napped. He snored, farted. I thought about my siblings and the old friends I'd put off seeing. Instead, I was enduring this. Still in the grip of jet lag, sleep also tried to claim me.

Wilde's shouting roused me with a start. His stacks of writing had vanished. I tried to magick his story back to the table, but couldn't. His rage turned to grief. I tried to console him, but again failed. He charged from the café. I hurried alongside him down Dawson Street and suggested we see a play. Over breakfast, I'd read a rave review for *The Lieutenant of Inishmore*. We could catch the matinee.

Wilde paused on Grafton Street to read a young man's cardboard sign, its bottom edge serrated. *If ten people give me two euro I'll have enough to get a bed tonight.*

When I first immigrated to Chicago, I couldn't believe the amount of homeless on the streets and the depths of their wretchedness. More, I couldn't comprehend how people blindly walked past them. All too soon, I had also turned numb. Now there were more and more homeless on the streets of Dublin and its crowds milled past, ignoring, normalizing.

"Tragic," Wilde said of the sign with contempt.

"May I?" I said to the young man, fishing a pen from my backpack. I turned the ripped cardboard over and demanded Wilde dictate. *Once, I was you. Someday, you could be me.* The young man's dirty fingers scrabbled at Wilde's words, as if trying to lift them off the cardboard. I saw a flash of him as a child, touching snow for the first time.

"What's your name?" I asked.

"Richie," he said, and laughed. "I'm thinking of changing it."

"Hiya, Richie," I said, handing him a twenty. "Please use it for shelter."

He promised, and thanked me, his head bowing repeatedly to a beat only he could hear.

"He's absolutely going to buy drugs, or at least drink. I know I would," Wilde said.

Inside the Gaiety, the green stage curtains parted. Wilde issued a startling sound twinning agony and euphoria. Throughout the performance, he repeatedly shouted "Bollocks," alternatively angry, contemptuous, impressed, aroused.

As we exited the theatre, he muttered, "Even at the best of times cats are a perversion."

On the walk back to the guesthouse, he stopped in front of his childhood home and placed his hand over his heart. Inside the park, in front of his monument, he adjusted his stiff penis.

Inside the pizzeria on Upper Grand Canal Street, we shared bruschetta and a beetroot salad with goat cheese and pomegranate seeds, the latter an act of God.

"He doesn't exist," Wilde said. "Spoiler, sorry."

We lamented the vinegary red wine. He said, "Wit, that's the only place tart belongs."

He demanded port and tiramisu. I wanted to get back to the guesthouse, and safety. Da and Mary had gotten along great until they started going outside together. They went from drinking themselves happy in pubs to falling down drunk on streets, to disappearing for days, to getting into altercations. I insisted Wilde skip dessert.

In my bedroom, I changed into flannel pajamas and messaged my three sons in our group chat. My eldest, James, responded first. *Hope you're having fun.* I played Tina Turner from my phone. My youngest, Danny, sent a thumbs up emoji. The middle child, PJ, might not respond for days. Wilde and I danced to "What's Love Got to Do With It."

He breathlessly declared, "You're going up in my estimation."

I shouted above the music. "Tell me the best is yet to come."

"The best is yet to come," he roared.

Mary had only obeyed Da for so long. I was determined to remain queen of Wilde. We danced, my subject and I. How we danced.

In bed, he folded himself against my back and locked his arm around my waist. I slept. How I slept.

၅⬯⬯⬯

In the morning, Wilde's side of the bed was empty. I remembered I'd started a higher dose of my antidepressant and wasn't supposed to drink alcohol, but the floaty effects were spectacular. I likely had that, the lingering haze of my sleeping tablets, and my twisted imagination to thank for Wilde's guest appearance. PJ messaged me back. *Take photos.* It was almost 4 a.m. in Brooklyn. *You okay?* I typed. I waited, but he didn't respond. Once more, sleep closed in.

In the early afternoon, I walked to my hair appointment. Along the way, I discovered St. Mary's church and felt compelled to enter. God or no God, I'd always loved churches—their stillness and sacredness. The thrum of hope.

I deposited every coin in my possession into one of several padlocked money boxes and burned an entire row of candles below St. Anthony, patron saint for the recovery of lost things.

"Thief!"

I turned around, expecting to find Wilde, but I was alone. Yet I felt a presence. Those long-ago skin-crawling sensations returned, during Da's first sightings of Mary and on realizing how wide his mind had split. He and I would get into shouting matches. Me saying Mary wasn't real, and him calling me a thief, trying to steal Mary from him. I rushed out to the street and into the cold, sharp air.

I arrived to the hair salon flustered and teary. The receptionist checked me in, her entire face smiling and her deep African accent powerful. She offered to take my jacket.

"I was mugged," I blurted.

"Jesus. When?"

"Just now, on the way here."

She rushed out from behind the reception desk and touched the top of my arm. "Are you okay?"

"I'll be fine, thank you." The relief of the lie was already fading and guilt was swooping in.

"Take a seat," she said, leading me to a white pleather chair. "Would you like tea? Black, green, mint, or chamomile?"

How far Ireland had come in the twenty-seven years since I'd left. "Mint, thank you."

She returned with the steaming mug of tea. "Would you like to reschedule your appointment? Because that would be no problem."

"I'm fine, really."

She moved behind me and spoke to my reflection in the mirror. "Just straight and sleek, yeah?" she said, placing her hands on my shoulders. My skin prickled, sending a fresh crawling sensation up my neck and over my scalp. I couldn't remember the last time anyone's touch had made me tingle.

She led me to the washbasin, my shoulders missing her warmth. Her head massage proved horribly weak. Maybe she felt the need to go gentle on me. I wanted to be worked on.

We returned to her station and she combed through my hair, tugging on the knots. "Did you get a good look at him?"

"What?"

"The mugger?"

"It was a woman." The lies had an appetite of their own.

"No way. Did she take much?"

"About a hundred euro." I had committed to the fallacy and couldn't stop.

"A hundred euro? Jesus, that's awful, that is. She'll have no luck." Several times she said it. *She'll have no luck.*

My phone pinged, a reply from PJ. *I'm good. Why?* I was relieved, and annoyed. *"Why?"*

"Are you at least going somewhere nice tonight?"

"No plans, really," I said, prolific now in deceit. She didn't need to know that I was meeting my siblings and their spouses for dinner.

The ordeal ended. I followed her back to the reception desk. "I'd love to not have to charge you," she said apologetically.

"That's okay, thanks," I said, pulling a roll of cash from my jeans pocket.

"Oh," she said, surprised.

I realized I should have used my credit card. I mumbled an excuse, only "after" and "ATM" clearly audible. Her eyes narrowed.

෨⊗෮

At dinner, inside the trendy, candlelit restaurant on Dame Street, we totaled a party of seven—my younger sister and her husband, my two older brothers and their wives, and me. Within minutes of meeting, we appeared entirely caught up. My gaze slyly tracked our waiter. When I finally caught his attention, I signaled for another rum and Coke. My sister looked down the table at me, concerned, questioning. In energetic, deflecting detail, I told them about the play at the Gaiety and afterward the delicious Italian dinner.

"You went alone?" my sister said.

"Yes," I said, only it felt like another lie.

I pushed away thoughts of the hair salon and continued drinking, no longer caring if they judged me. The imperative was to douse my dishonesty, and the fear of inheritance.

Most of the next day, anxiety and a ringing hangover pinned me to the bed. Finally, parched and famished, I hauled myself out of the guesthouse—freshly convinced I was a lot of things, including lonely and an attention-seeker, but I wasn't mad. I struggled over the now familiar streets of Ballsbridge, feeling wholly tender, as if my body had been beaten black and blue. A walking hematoma. The first time I heard that word, I was fifteen. The doctor was describing the massive bruise on Da's hip after falling down our stairs. Da claimed Ma had pushed him, his voice turning shrill with fright and paranoia. The police interviewed Ma, my siblings, and me. Next, the psychiatrist took her turn with us. Ma reluctantly signed the papers, committing Da to Grangegorman. His stay lasted months, and when he returned home Mary was gone. As I passed the Grand Canal Hotel, I could still hear him wailing for her.

I continued on aimlessly, chancing unfamiliar streets in search of something beyond hydration and food. Arriving at the docklands, I stopped short at the edge of the plaza, stunned by the glittering waterway, state-of-the-art glass theatre, and the revamped redbrick and cast-iron warehouses. For a fog-brained moment, I thought I was back in Chicago's financial district. I followed the savory drift from a large, fancy-looking supermarket named *fresh*. At the expansive meal counter, I eyed the roasted meats and vegetables, mounds of stuffing and mashed potatoes, and trays of thick gravy and sauces. Overwhelmed, I moved to the soup and salad buffet, then to the shop's deli, butchers, bakery, and aisle after aisle of tantalizing foods, wanting so much and taking nothing.

I paused at the supermarket's café and the rows of brightly colored donuts behind spotless glass. I could be standing inside Firecakes Donuts in Lincoln Park. There was a time when there was a world of difference between Ireland and America, but with each passing year, I saw more of the sameness creeping in. It was tempting to think I could resettle here, but the craggy island dredged up too much for me to stay permanently. I returned to the soups and ladled my fill. *Homemade*, the sign promised.

In the last days of Da's life, Mary returned. "I thought I'd killed her," he told me through the phone, his voice carrying from Dublin to Chicago. "She says she's sorry."

"For what?"

"She hurt a lot of people."

I was still trying to work up to something when he said, "Would you forgive her?"

"That's up to you," I said, wondering if he was asking something else. I've often questioned, since, if he somehow knew that would be our last conversation.

*Each man kills the thing he loves.* It was a Wilde quote I expected to see on one of those pillars inside the park, but it was excluded. Perhaps I wasn't the only one who didn't understand it. I rushed the chicken noodle soup inside me, tasting mercy, and yet again wondered what Wilde had loved and killed. Maybe it was God. Maybe that's why Wilde said He didn't exist. Regardless, it was wrong of him to implicate everyone in the same murderous act. It seemed far more true that we kill parts inside those we should love the most, ourselves included.

# F Is for Something

FATHER QUINLAN LOWERED THE TYPED LETTER to the kitchen table. It stated Bishop Clemens himself would arrive that afternoon to hand down the priest's sentence. He'd lost count of the number of times he'd read the letter over the past week, and still he couldn't absorb it. He had given the Church forty-seven years of dedicated, selfless service, and they planned to force him into retirement regardless. They would most likely stick him at something token and useless in yet another parish, answering the church phone and doling out signed Mass cards.

Shivering, he pushed the remains of his late breakfast aside, the milk congealed at the top of his tea like cataract clouding a large, brown eye. He excused himself—his housekeeper, Moira, didn't as much as look up from scrubbing the small saucepan at the sink—and hurried out.

Upstairs, he reached inside his wardrobe for his navy wool cardigan. Instead, his hand strayed to the shoulder of his once-white linen suit, a remnant from his missionary stint in Nigeria, thirty years back, when he was young and vital. He'd never before or since wavered in his vocation except for those few months abroad, when he couldn't convince himself those villagers needed his interference or his God. They had more than enough faith, goodness, and joy in their own ways.

He held the stiff white suit against his chest in the full-length mirror, startled by the gaunt, wizened face staring back from above the hanger's metal hook. Grooves sliced his forehead and his cheeks looked hollowed out. The black sub-layer of his hair beneath the puff of white frizz made him think of earth and bone. Inside, he felt decades younger. What was the name of that village outside Laos, and its noble chief? Both names circled the edge of his mind. They would come back to him. Give him a second. In the mirror, the effort to remember made his head tremble.

The chief had died many years back. Father Quinlan had hoped to return to Nigeria for his funeral, the two having forged a deep friendship during their short time together, but the Church wouldn't allow him to travel, citing the cost, visa paperwork, and his pressing duties at home. He'd obeyed, despite his disappointment and grief. Of course he had. He'd followed the Archdiocese's every decree without question for almost five decades. That heavy feeling came over him again, as if he were turning to concrete.

He returned to the kitchen. Moira stood next to the light of the window, darning his black sock, as though it was the year 1912 and not 2012. On seeing him, she snapped the line of black wool with her crooked teeth and stabbed the needle into a pincushion. Her thick nails and sharp incisors, her height and leathery skin, made him think of those enormous lizards in Nigeria, sneaky, rapid creatures measuring anywhere between five and nine feet. The red-brown of Moira's eyes also recalled the reptiles, brazen beings that still sometimes scrabbled into his dreams and hissed at him, their long, forked tongues flickering.

"What is it you want, Father?" Her scowl made him feel like a muddied dog that had strayed into her house.

"Just helping myself to a mug of tea."

"I'll get it, Father. You sit down there now and stay out of my way." She about-turned and banged two saucepans together at the sink for no other reason, it seemed, than to vex him. She had to be the rowdiest woman ever let loose in a house. She clanged the copper kettle onto the enamel range. "What did you do with the good china teapot? I need it for the bishop's visit today."

He hitched his shoulders, feigning innocence.

"And where are my reading glasses?" she went on. "I know I left them on the windowsill."

He'd had great sport in recent days, hiding things and cutting at her confidence in her faculties, just as she regularly did to him. "You're awfully forgetful, Father. You're confused, Father. I've told you all this already, Father."

She fixed him with her cold eyes. "I can't imagine why you'd play these games with me, Father. Not you of all people."

*Not you of all people* buzzed in his head.

He retired to the front room, the heaviness in his limbs and chest worsening. The sounds of Moira sweeping the kitchen floor carried, the needles of the broom scratching the linoleum and its head banging the base of the cabinets with relish. What if he hadn't entered the priesthood? If he'd married instead and it was his wife bustling about the kitchen? Next, she would prepare lunch—triangles of salty tomato and cucumber sandwiches, and thick slices of buttered sultana cake—while he settled by the warmth of the range and tackled the *Indo's* crossword. They would sit and eat together at the kitchen table, the harmonious quiet interrupted by the odd question, pleasant murmur, or update on the children (three girls, all grown). Full, content, they would take an afternoon nap, his body fitted to the bony curves of her back like two halves of a whole, and their breaths a single refrain. He clapped his hand to his brow. It was no use. He only wanted the one life and it was being taken from him.

He checked the clock on the mantelpiece, the bishop's arrival drawing ever nearer. In the mirror over the fireplace, a large nerve in his cheek pulsed, like a finger moving back and forth beneath his skin. He already knew he was to be banished and didn't see the point of the bishop's visit. Unless it was an opportunity to convince His Lordship to grant him clemency? He resumed pacing up and down in front of the empty hearth until he was seized with an idea. He would go down to the village in this, the eleventh hour, and find some good deed to perform, some hope or faith or kindness to kindle. Anything to prove to his parishioners and Bishop Clemens that he was still useful.

At the front door, his courage wavered. The whole parish knew his failings and his fate. Movement sounded behind him, the unmistakable drag of Moira's slippers over the carpet, the gray footwear like two flattened squirrels. The threat of her trumped his apprehension and prodded him out onto the empty road. Once he cleared a safe distance from the house, he slowed his gait in the cold gray morning, his every sense alert to how he might accomplish some stroke of heroism. Two tall lines of ash trees flanked him, the branches still magnificent despite their winter nakedness. The Atlantic's chill nipped his face, biting down to his bones. He rolled his shoulders, his teeth chattering, and pulled his coat collar up to his ears.

He passed the primary school, the building little more than a house-sized bungalow and painted in Mother Mary blue. Navy uniformed children played ball and rope in the schoolyard while the two women teachers stood bundled up in layers of grays and greens. He waved and called out to the merry group with perhaps too much animation, eager to appear full of life.

He struggled to drum up the teachers' names. Perhaps it was only his imagination, but their greeting seemed cool, guarded. The children, hard at play, didn't pay him any heed. In his five months as their parish priest, he hadn't gotten out and about much, needing to recover from the distress and humiliation of his transfer from Kilmaine's large, bustling parish to this tiny, dormant village. So stagnant it wasn't even a dot on the map. Before the bishop's letter, he'd believed he had all the time in the world to make his mark on this place.

The sheep on the hill bleated. A sensation stirred his chest, like his own lament calling back to them. Yet surely it wasn't too late for him to redeem himself. He had plans to start a church choir; recruit young gospel readers; and initiate more activities in the village hall: drama, bingo, and family game nights. What was the other big thing he was going to do? The thing he had felt so excited about last night in bed he couldn't sleep? Ack—he had better remember before the bishop arrived. Had best impress His Lordship with his various schemes, and more so his renewed energy and clarity.

He would, all right, have to admit to Bishop Clemens he had acted erratically this past year. Losing house and car keys, mislaying church donations, appearing late at Mass, and even, God help him, forgetting to show altogether to some services. The new rites dictated by the Vatican, they were another snare. For the life of him, he couldn't remember the revised words for the Mass or the sacraments and still had to read from the vinyl cheat sheets on the altar. Such oversights were all minor matters, though, and nothing that greater discipline and concentration couldn't fix. He felt much less willing, however, to broach the Tynan tragedy with Bishop Clemens. His heart drew back into his chest, as if trying to hide from the morning chill and his growing dread.

⁧☙⁩

Father Quinlan entered the speck of a village and crossed the road toward Horan's whitewashed shop. It and Fogarty's blackwashed pub amounted to the grand total of businesses in the village proper. A scatter of homes stood within spitting distance of the shop and pub, and the lone thatched cottage, with its tangerine door and manicured hedge, held court at the fork of the main road—the historic property in foreclosure and sitting idle since before the priest's arrival, a sobering centerpiece of the village's decline.

He arrived at the shop, spotting Nancy Horan standing behind the counter. He recalled her fervent murmurs through the confessional grille, tortured admissions of her rage against the life the Lord had laid out for her. Widowed in her late thirties, she remained a single parent to six children and worried for the survival of her shop, and her sanity. He entered through the open door. Nancy's attention remained fixed on the ledger on the counter, her pen poised and her forehead pleated. He scanned the space, relieved to find it empty, and closed the door.

Nancy startled, her hand rushing to her chest. "Oh hello, Father. You gave me a fright."

"I'm sorry." He stiffened, rattled by the strain in his voice.

"Is everything all right, Father?"

"I—" He could only shake his head.

"Is Moira not with you, Father? I don't think you're supposed to be out and about on your own?" Her voice betrayed scolding, impatience. His hopes of finding an ally in her started to fade.

The shop door opened. He jumped backward, as though caught doing something he shouldn't. Betty Something or Other entered, the woman sixtyish and stiff-backed. She squinted at Nancy and him, her hair the color of wet hay. He busied himself, pretending to browse the shelves. More customers came and went, casting sideways glances in his direction. Betty whispered on with Nancy, seeming in no hurry to leave.

"Are you sure you're all right there, Father?" Nancy called out.

"I was hoping to finish our chat, Mrs. Horan, in private?"

"I'm sorry, Father, this isn't a good time. Is Moira above in the house? I can phone her—"

Betty insisted she would man the shop while he and Nancy retreated to the back kitchen. He caught the look Nancy aimed at Betty, more annoyance than gratitude.

Nancy hurried about her cluttered kitchen, carrying dirty dishes to the sink and gathering toys and clothes into baskets. "You'll have to excuse the mess, Father."

He indicated the chair opposite him at the table. "Sit, please. There's no need to fuss on my account."

She perched on the chair, looking like a sprinter waiting for the starting shot. "You'll take a cup of tea." She sprang from the seat, talking in a constant stream about the weather, recession, and exodus of the nation's young, her voice fast and falsetto. He only half listened, the heat from the range sending him into a sweet drowsy state.

A boy, aged about five, ran into the room, rousing the priest. He dragged after him a wooden dog on a string, the toy mounted on wheels and the tip of the animal's tail painted nut brown. Nancy introduced her youngest, Thomas.

"Is he friendly?" Father Quinlan asked.

"Well of course," Nancy said, sounding baffled. "He's a good little lad."

Father Quinlan frowned. He had meant, in jest, the toy dog. Did she, everyone, think he was doting to that degree? He swallowed the fullness in his throat and removed the coins from his trouser pocket, motioned for the boy to come closer. "Fetch me the *Indo*, son, and get yourself a treat with what's left."

Nancy poured from the stainless steel teapot, its fat body coated in a greasy film. She pushed the plate of plain biscuits closer, her smile as watery as the tea. "Don't be shy, Father."

"I'd like you to do something for me, please?"

"If I can," she said, alarm rising off her like the vapors from the tea.

"Bishops Clemens is coming to see me today at three o'clock. Perhaps you'd be kind enough to stop by and speak with him on my behalf? A character reference, if you will."

She shook her head, her face flaming crimson. "I don't really know you, though, do I, Father? What I do know is that everyone, the bishop included, is aware you've worked long and hard enough, and now it's time for you to take a well-earned rest."

Panic surged from his stomach through his chest and into his head, a riptide. "Please, it would mean a great deal."

Her eyes dampened. "I'm so sorry, Father. I don't think it would help."

His gaze dropped to his smudged reflection in the filmy teapot, like something blotted out. He rushed from the room, and the shop. He would not allow the bishop, anyone, to erase him.

Outside, he spotted Tynan's green tractor in the distance, lumbering over the far road in that trembling way of oversized vehicles. It must be old Tynan himself or the second son behind the wheel. He saw another flash of Joe Tynan pinned beneath the tractor, the blood pumping from his head and turning the soil to muck. He wiped his brow, as if to rid his mind of the image, and beelined to Fogarty's.

When he entered the toasty pub, every head in the place turned toward the open door. Their attention, and his oversized wool coat, made him feel smothered. He'd bought the coat a couple of years ago in a charity shop in Kilmaine, back when he'd started to no longer feel secure in himself and the world. There was always something he wasn't doing or remembering right, and someone forever checking up on him, trying to catch him out in his confusion. It helped, if only a little, to wrap himself in the too-big coat.

He sat on a barstool at the dull cherry counter. Fogarty delivered a Jameson in a well-scratched glass, a single cube of ice floating in the jigger of amber. The publican had the looks of a rock star, with his lean build, shoulder-length silver hair, and penchant for bright shirts opened one button too many. "Father, we don't normally get the pleasure."

"I don't get too much of it myself these days," Father Quinlan said. Fogarty laughed, a deep rumble. The scatter of punters stared.

"Well share the joke, can't you?" said a young lad sitting at the end of the counter.

Father Quinlan's attention drifted to the oil painting behind the bar—a portrait of a fisherman standing knee-deep in a rushing green river, about to cast his line.

"Have you ever fished, Father?" Fogarty said.

Father Quinlan shook his head. The village in Nigeria was located right on the river. The chief had offered to take him fishing many times, but he'd refused. There was something especially cruel about how fish were baited and killed. The unsuspecting creature opened its mouth to sustenance, only to be hooked by sharp pain and dragged from the water to a brutal undoing.

"Me neither," Fogarty said. "Fishing is like golf, it takes years of practice and patience, and I wouldn't have the inclination for either." When the priest didn't respond, he went on. "Priests, you're fishers of men, isn't that it?"

He served Father Quinlan a second Jameson and single cube of ice. The priest stared at his empty glass, blinking hard. He didn't remember drinking the whiskey but could feel its fire in his chest and taste its smoky tang. He lifted the second drink to his face and breathed deep, determined to be an active participant in the downing of this one.

He finished, and asked Fogarty the time. The bar's clock had only one arm. Fogarty checked his wristwatch, rare now in the age of mobile phones. "Ten after two."

Father Quinlan's head cramped. He had less than an hour to save himself. With a tiny jolt, the name he'd been grasping at returned. "Minbabi."

"What's that, Father?" Fogarty asked.

"Minbabi." That was the name of the Nigerian chief, his old friend. "It means 'Great One.'" He heard *Fa-dah* at his ear, as if the chief were standing right next to him. He waited to hear more, but there was only the chatter from the punters, a mournful ballad from the radio, and the fleshy squelch from Fogarty squeezing a lemon.

Fogarty glanced at the priest's second empty glass. "Can I get you something else, Father? A coffee, or water?"

"No, thank you." Father Quinlan closed his eyes. *Fa-dah*. Minbabi wasn't so much saying his name as issuing a command.

"Wakey, wakey, Father." The voice belonged to the young lad at the end of the bar.

Father Quinlan glanced at the fellow's ring finger, finding it thick and naked. His eyes jumped to the painting of the fisherman and back again, his heart pounding so hard he could feel his pulse in his ears. "Son, have you ever thought of joining the priesthood?" The lad laughed harshly. "What about one of your friends?" Father Quinlan asked, his eyes raking the other men.

"You are off your rocker, aren't you?" The lad and his friends laughed.

Fogarty slapped a wet towel on the counter next to the lad's elbow, sounding a *splat*. "Have some manners."

Father Quinlan was in water, getting pulled down by the waves. Fogarty came out from behind the counter and threaded his arm through the priest's, easing him up from the barstool. "Come on, Father, let's get you home." Father Quinlan shook off Fogarty's grip. He was grand. About time he was getting on, though. Something important he needed to do. Something. It would come to him.

As he pushed through the doors of the pub, that mouthy lad spoke up. "If I change my mind about getting the collar, I'll let you know." More laughter. Like hyenas, some would say. But Father Quinlan had heard hyenas in Africa, and their noises sounded less like laughter and more like chattering pleas. He stopped on the side of the road, waiting and watching. Praying. There was nothing. No feat to perform, no miracle to make, no soul to save. He stayed put, his eyes peeled.

∞

Moira's sharp voice beat him back into the house. He sat in the kitchen next to the fiery blast from the range, stomping his leaden feet on the linoleum and breathing heat into what felt like phantom hands.

"What were you at out there, anyway?" Moira said.

He couldn't remember exactly, but something. Something. His arm shot straight up, punching overhead. "No surrender."

Moira pulled on the rigid limb, making him think of those squeaky handles on the water pumps in Nigeria. "Upstairs with you quick, Father, and brush your teeth. You smell like a distillery and His Lordship will be here any minute."

His stomach tightened. How could he have forgotten the bishop? His eyes cut to the clock over the fridge, its white hands marking the hour Jesus had died on the cross. He hurried out, and to the front door.

Moira let out a little yelp. "Where are you going?"

He continued outside, her screech chasing him. He needed to play the perfect host and greet the bishop on his arrival. He moved over the gravel, a sound like the snap of wishbones. Moira pulled on his arm, demanding he return inside. She dragged him as far as the house, but rather than enter, he closed the front door.

"What did you do, Father? You've locked us out."

He laughed, the sound explosive, and pulled his keys from his trousers pocket, dangled them in front of her horrified face. The keys slipped from his grasp and he snatched them up, grazing his knuckles on the gravel. He sucked on the wettest cut, encouraged by his saltiness and how freely his blood flowed. A little Fiat the color of saffron turned into the yard. Moira snapped the keys and opened the front door, guided him toward the stairs.

✺

Father Quinlan entered the living room. Moira stood over Bishop Clemens, handing him a steaming cup of tea on a saucer. Father Quinlan strode across the room, his hair combed and his mouth coated in spearmint.

Bishop Clemens stood up, alarmed. "Matthew, your hand?"

Father Quinlan ignored the threads of blood trickling toward his wrist and kissed the bishop's ruby ring. "Your Lordship."

Moira pressed a paper napkin to his scraped knuckles, rounds of red blooming on the white tissue. He pushed her hand away. Bishop Clemens indicated the two armchairs next to the roaring fire. "Shall we?"

"That will be all, Moira," Father Quinlan said.

Moira looked to the bishop for confirmation. He nodded. She shuffled toward the door.

"How are you holding up, Matthew?" the bishop began, his face pained. "This is difficult, I know. Everything's gotten to be a bit too much for you, hasn't it?" He continued in soothing tones, revealing the full extent of Father Quinlan's fall. The priest was being placed in a nursing home in Dublin. "You'll be a man of leisure. You won't know yourself."

Father Quinlan rushed to his feet, as if the chair had ejected him, and charged from the room, ordering His Lordship to follow.

Father Quinlan reached the church and looked back at the bishop's clumsy advance over the gravel yard. He continued inside, and climbed onto the red-carpeted altar. Bishop Clemens stopped midway down the center aisle, breathless, heaving.

Father Quinlan opened his arms wide. "Your Lordship, in God's own house, tell me again how you're going to strip me of everything and leave me to rot."

"Calm yourself, Father, there's the good man. Let's go back to the house."

He rushed at the bishop, grabbed his cold, fleshy wrist, and pulled him toward the confessional boxes. "You'll absolve me of my sins and failings, allow me to start over."

The bishop protested. Father Quinlan opened the confessional's center door and urged His Lordship inside. Bishop Clemens refused. Father Quinlan entered the confessional's side section and pulled the narrow door closed. He sank to his knees in the dark and waited.

At last the bishop entered the main confessional, the wooden seat creaking under his weight. He slid back the brass grille cover in the thin wall between them.

Father Quinlan brought his face close to the dull divider. "Bless me, Your Lordship, for I have sinned—"

He had missed the turn on the road to the Tynan farm that terrible day. Lost, he drove down one boreen after another and over the maze of bog and byways, trying to find his way out. Joe's younger brother tracked him down and drove them at alarming speed to the scene of the accident. Father Quinlan could almost hear the churn of the young man's heart. Gerry. Maybe that was his name. Joe Tynan died just seconds before his brother and Father Quinlan arrived in a squeal of brakes, and before he could be given the Last Rites. Father Quinlan slapped his head with both hands.

"Stop that, Father, you'll hurt yourself," Bishop Clemens said.

How had he managed to get lost that day? He'd traveled that route many times prior, to give Holy Communion to Mrs. Tynan, the woman bedbound for weeks following a surgery that had gone awry. There was more, though, and that must be what had sealed this unthinkable fate. He'd felt so distraught by his incompetence that afternoon, so rattled after getting lost and arriving too late, he'd stuttered and stumbled through the final sacrament, forgetting the words of the Last Rites while Joe's blood cooled.

He lifted his tear-stained face. "Absolve me, Your Lordship, I beg you. Give me another chance."

⌇⌇

Moira entered the darkened living room, only the Tiffany-style lamp casting its weak glow. "Will you take your tea now, Father?"

He turned back to the window, dusk enveloping the rows of beech trees. A scrap of schooling returned. *I think that I shall never see a poem lovely as a tree.*

"Father?"

He startled, having forgotten Moira. "What is it?"

"Your tea, Father? You must be hungry."

"No, thank you. I won't have anything this evening."

She frowned. "No tea, Father?"

"That's right. You can leave for the day."

"But it's not yet six o'clock. I've still plenty to do—"

"I said that will be all. In fact, you don't ever have to come back."

"What are you saying, Father?"

"I'd like the house to myself for the short time that's left to me here."

Stricken, she clasped her hands at her fallen-in stomach. "Nonsense, Father, you can't possibly manage on your own. Besides, what have I to go home to? What else have I to do?" She sounded as plaintive as the sheep on the hill.

He crossed the room, stunned by her distress. She was trembling, a leaf afraid it would be ripped from the tree. "Don't mind me. I'll take my tea after all, and will see you in the morning. Everything's as it was."

"Right so, Father, that's more like it." Her relief allowed the air in the room to move again. As she exited, she flipped on the overhead light.

He returned to the window, his collared reflection filling the glass. He stared at himself, understanding that he'd been gifted this exchange with Moira, and with Minbabi's return earlier. Man and mirror nodded at each other, forging a pact. He would continue to find ways to priest, acts however small, for however long.

# ANY WONDER LEFT

MY TWO SISTERS AND I work throughout the day, clearing out our parents' home. The easiest room to tackle is the kitchen, there great satisfaction to be had in throwing away the useless and expired: food, condiments, flyers, paid bills, and inkless pens. The hardest space to brave is Dad's bedroom. Here, especially, my sisters and I argue over what should stay or go, right down to his medications, faded bookie receipts, and dusty shoes. In the end we throw away almost everything except photographs, Granddad's blackthorn walking stick that Dad treasured, and the newspaper comic strips that Dad collected over decades.

By mid-afternoon, fourteen fat plastic rubbish bags line both sides of our parents' driveway. The three bags on the right will go to the charity shop, and the eleven on the left to the city dump. A neighbor, Mrs. Reilly, barrels through the front gate and stands scowling at the bags, her disapproval as obvious as her drooping breasts. "Yis didn't start into all that already?" she says.

Dad is dead two weeks.

"Had to be done sometime," I sing out. She looks at me like my ruthless head has turned three hundred and sixty degrees. She knows I staged a similar swift erasure of our mother's belongings last spring, just a few weeks after she died. My smile remains defiant. Mrs. Reil-ly's expression shifts to a kind of pity, as if she's remembered I'm not only an adult orphan now, but also a young widow.

"I'll let yis get back to it," she says, unable to keep the lingering disdain out of her voice. She turns on her heel, her ankles pale and plump as halibut.

My sisters and I return inside, getting away from the black bags sweating in the afternoon heat. It's as if the sun has gone rogue, defying winter. The idea that nature is staging its own rebellion is strangely comforting, given my own pushback against everything that's happened.

⁊◯

In the kitchen, over copious cups of tea, my sisters and I reminisce about our parents, childhood, and the neighbors, issuing bursts of laughter and sometimes sniffling. My sisters swipe at their red-rimmed eyes with bunched, flaking tissues. Beyond the French doors, birds swoop in and out of the back garden, pecking uselessly at the red metal feeder. The empty birdseed sack is in a black bag out front. I imagine it was one of the last things Dad did, refilling the feeder. I make a note to pick up more seeds.

In the nearest corner of the garden, the two gray, ring-necked doves remain perched on a bottom branch of the apple tree. Dad bought the young tree in Aldi a few years back. I'd told him it would never grow, and most certainly never bear fruit. Mum, shaking her gray-blond head, sounded a small laugh. "That man. He might as well have flushed the five euro down the toilet."

When the tree grew and its first green apple appeared, Dad rubbed his hands together with delight. "Didn't I tell yis."

He further gloated over the two collared doves stationed on the lower branches of the tree, insisting they were the same pair that had visited his garden every day for years.

"How can you know?" I reasoned. "They could be any of thousands of doves."

"They're the same two," he said, his voice thick with tenderness, reverence.

I pour more tea. Of the four chairs at the table, it's no accident that I'm sitting in one of the two neutral seats. Tina sits in Mum's chair and Isabel sits in Dad's. When we sell the house, they will likely want to keep this table and chairs and most of everything else that remains. They're welcome to the lot. I don't want any such reminders. Mementos are nothing more than evidence of the missing.

We discuss how to get Dad's belongings to the dump. The haul is much bigger than we expected and will require at least three trips in Tina's car. "I don't even know where the dump is," she says. At thirty-two, and with those downturned lips and large brown eyes that always look damp, she still holds hard to her status as the baby of the family.

"It's not called the dump anymore. It's some sanitized name now, a civic center or something," Isabel says. She's the most attractive of the three of us, with her long chestnut hair, smooth, sallow skin, and jutting cheekbones. At thirty-five, she still cannot drive and refuses to learn—too afraid of losing control of the vehicle, and of not being in control of other drivers. I doubt, though, she knows the kind of powerlessness that makes your lungs feel trapped inside plastic, or the terror that makes your heart feel like it will detonate.

Tina volunteers their husbands to transport the bags. Both men are at home, minding their respective children. "It's too late today, but I can check to see if the dump, or whatever it's called now, is open tomorrow."

"No husbands needed, and no point in dragging this out," I say with an edge. "I'll take care of it."

Tina and Isabel exchange a look that conveys both sympathy and irritation. At thirty-eight, I am the eldest and have always played the part of the capable, bossy sister much too well.

"You don't even have a car," Tina says. Her cheeks flare red. "Oh God, sorry. That was a stupid thing to say."

Brendan's and my car was smashed in the collision, a write-off. "I'm going to get it sorted. I'll be back in a bit."

Ignoring their protests and apologies, I walk out of the kitchen, and the murmuring house.

The sign that had stood on the neighborhood green for months, advertising a handyman, is gone. I scan my surroundings, disbelieving, angry. Some unseen power keeps messing with me.

A tall, lean man walks a lively King Charles along the tarmac pathway circling the green. I approach, thinking he's likely a regular. Up close, he's not as old as I'd first thought, maybe in his late fifties. There's still something handsome about his rugged face and pale blue eyes. He confirms I'm not mistaken and that there was a sign for a handyman. He looks about us, also mystified by its disappearance. We shouldn't feel so surprised. The world over, things—people—are here one moment and gone the next.

"Is it a big job you need doing?" he asks.

I tell him about the bags of my dead father's belongings. "I'd really like rid of them today."

He shakes his head, his hair dyed the brown of a bird's nest. "Good luck finding someone to do that run for you at this hour."

The base of my throat buzzes. "Thanks anyway," I say, turning to leave. The King Charles jumps up on my legs, his sharp nails scratching the back of my knee. No one since Brendan has touched such an intimate part of me, or made me feel much of anything.

The man tugs on the dog's leash. "No, Frankie."

Dad's name was Frank. I almost tell the stranger, but don't. Some stuff sounds made up. Like how Mum, Dad, and Brendan died in the same year.

"I have a friend with a truck, and I think he'd do it for you nice and handy. Let me see if he's around. How much can I say you'll give him?"

"How about fifty euro?" I say, hoping it's in the realm of a fair price.

He looks dubious. "He'll have to pay dump fees, remember."

"Eighty, then?"

"That might work." He walks toward the middle of the green, his phone to his ear, and quickly returns. "Sorry, no answer." He taps the side of the phone to his thin lips. A mustache would give him more of a mouth. "I can make this happen. Leave it with me."

We walk off the green together and onto the street, me thanking him repeatedly. He types Dad's address and my mobile number into his phone.

"You're a star." I extend my hand. "Nicola."

We shake, his touch warm. "Eamon." He promises to recruit a couple of lads with a van from Cabra and says he'll escort them to Dad's house himself. "We can be there in fifteen, twenty minutes."

My gratitude jumps to suspicion. How can he drum up lads with a van in Cabra of all places, and at such short notice? My pulse quickens, as though a wind has picked up inside me, driving my blood faster. "I'm putting you to too much trouble. Please don't worry about it. I'll figure something else out."

"It's no bother, and trust me, I only ever do what I want." The bite to his voice and chill in his glacier-blue eyes make me believe him.

Eamon pulls up outside our parents' house in a gray BMW. A white Ford Transit trails him, three lads filling the front passenger seat. I rush outside and close the front door behind me, not wanting them to see into the house, and maybe whet their appetite for more that they can take. My sisters watch from the bottom of the living room window, both crouched on the carpet, peeping out like kids. They are horrified that I've given a questionable stranger my phone number and our dead parents' address. Worse, I'm entrusting him with the disposal of Dad's belongings.

The three lads jump from the van with alarming purpose and quick-march up the driveway. They are dark-haired, stocky, and already have a certain savagery etched into their young faces. I point at the long row of bags on the left, smiling hard. "Just take everything on this side, please." My voice smacks of fake, fearful cheer.

Eamon appears next to me. "Good news. They agreed to do the job for fifty euro."

"Thanks, but we said eighty. Let's stick to that." I pull the four folded twenties from my jeans pocket, anxious not to piss off the youngfellas and risk them returning, looking for their full due.

I hand over Dad's money. During our clearing blitz, my sisters and I found over three hundred euro that he'd hidden inside various ornaments and a fat sock deep in his nightstand drawer, saving the money for never.

"Fair is fair," I add automatically, echoing something Dad often said and which I now disbelieve more than ever. There is no such thing as fairness—only luck, bad luck, and worse luck.

Eamon adds the notes to his thick money clip.

In a matter of minutes, the lads have all eleven bags thrown into the back of the van. I thank them yet again, breaking records for the depths of insincerity. They climb into the vehicle and look out from the front seat, their craggy faces blank. I shiver, realizing they are waiting for Eamon to signal their next move.

My need to supervise the sendoff turns urgent. Not least because these lads might fire the bags into a ditch, saving themselves the spin across town and pocketing the entire eighty euro. "Would it be all right if I followed them to the dump?" I blurt, thinking to borrow Tina's car.

Eamon nods, his slight lips pursed. "I don't see why not. I can take you."

"No," I say too fast, that wind again whipping the blood around my veins. His brow knits, and I rush to add, "You've done more than enough already."

"I insist." The clouded look leaves him. His blue eyes glitter with mischief. "Besides, those lads drive like maniacs at the best of times. They're a nightmare altogether when they're being followed."

"It's too much," I say, a nervous tremble in my voice.

He smiles with just a hint of cruelty. "If I didn't know better, I'd say you were scared." He lifts his chin toward the trio in the van. "Is it them?" He looks right into my eyes. "Or is it me?"

Despite how much I'm shaking, I do my best to stride toward his car with a spine of oak, and sit into the shiny vehicle with as much grace as possible. A voice in my head demands to know what I think I'm doing. I imagine my sisters are wondering the same, and half expect them to charge from the house. Eamon slides behind the driver's wheel, chuckling. "All right then."

My phone pings, a worried text from Tina. I type back reassurances.

As we drive, Eamon tells me he's seventy years old. I can't hide my surprise. "You look great."

"I can assure you it's not from easy living." He tells me he made and lost fortunes, and served eight years in Mountjoy for tax evasion. "The only thing those bastards in CAB could pin on me." It takes me a second to register that he's talking about the Criminal Assets Bureau. Just before Christmas, he continues, a masked gunman assassinated his brother-in-law on the street in broad daylight, a gangland revenge murder. "At least I'm still above ground."

"Wow," I say, hearing how ridiculous I am. I consider jumping from the car the next time we stop at a traffic light.

"Prison gave me lots of time to think. I read all sorts of books, philosophy mostly. I'm not the man I was. I'd never again do the things I did."

The silence stretches. I try not to think about the things he might have done.

"You?" he asks. "What's your story?"

"Well, nothing like yours," I say, not intending to be funny, but he laughs, firing from deep in his stomach.

He wants to know if I'm married, if I have kids, and where I live. I aim for vague but not antagonizing—you don't not answer his kind—and tell him no, no, and on the other side of town.

"Nothing wrong with a quiet life," he says.

There's so much I could say to that, but don't. Like how my life has taken to screaming.

We arrive at the dump, now called a civic amenity site. It couldn't be further from my memories of the place. As a girl, I'd gone here with Dad when we got rid of our rusted bathtub and the broken washing machine. The stink had hit us long before the mountains of rot and ruin came into view, and while I expected the skittering rats, I could never have prepared myself for their sheer number, like black, moving hills. I hadn't expected to see so much color amid the dark debris, either—blots of reds, pinks, yellows, and blues.

The amenity site is surrounded by metal railing topped with barbed wire. Inside stands a village of gray, corrugated warehouses splashed with the mill of yellow-vested workers. Eamon shifts on the driver's seat, his expression knotty. He's perhaps having flashbacks to Mountjoy Prison, and could take his trauma out on me. I should never have come here.

At the site's entrance, a man in a white hardhat and orange vest grips a clipboard and speaks with the lads in the van. Eamon's car idles behind them, and I watch with growing alarm as the exchange turns heated. The driver rushes from the van and plods wide-legged toward Eamon, like he's fresh from bare horseback riding.

"They want to know what's in the fucking bags. Everything has to be divided into all different kinds of shit, recycling and wha' not," he says.

My mood plunges. It would take an age to sort everything in those bags into their respective piles. "It's just rubbish," I say, protesting, pleading. A horrible feeling rushes me. That's the bulk of my dad I'm talking about.

"Leave it to me," Eamon says, exiting the car. He talks with the gatekeeper, their heads close together, and slips him money. As he walks back to the car, the gatekeeper gives the driver directions, his arm outstretched. The van peels away. Eamon returns to the car, and we roll forward.

"I'll pay you back," I say, not wanting to be any deeper in his debt.

"Don't worry about it," he says.

I receive another text from Tina, demanding an update. I thumb a rushed reply, *at dump all well*, and hope that is indeed the case.

The BMW snakes along the main path and past the metal warehouses, columns of compressed, multicolored waste, and mounds of plastic recycling. The computer screens are piled high and wide in a rectangular block like a huge, many-faced robot. We reach the landfill, where there's another gatekeeper, this man younger, blockier. He waves the van and Eamon through.

While Eamon and I remain inside his car, the three lads pull the bags of Dad's belongings from the back of the Transit and toss them onto the heaps of mangled waste like they're nothing.

"That's it, don't look away," Eamon says. It's as if he knows I'm fighting the urge. A chill scissors my back. It was Brendan who discarded Mum's belongings, sparing Dad, my sisters, and me from the task. Six months later, while he was driving home from work, a car going in the wrong direction on the motorway crashed into him head-on.

In the days after his funeral, I stripped our home, getting rid of everything from the bottles in the drinks cabinet to the last stick of furniture, emptying the place of him, and him and me.

Family and friends despaired. *Would you not wait? You might regret it. You shouldn't do anything so soon, let alone this. Is it not a terrible waste?* I ignored them and isolated myself, a hedgehog curled into a spiky ball.

Much more than my favorite ornaments, furniture, and kitchenware—more than our photographs, the jewelry Brendan had given me, and the ticket stubs we'd saved from every concert we'd attended together—it was his phone with his voicemail recording that proved the hardest to part with. After selling and donating everything I could, I hired a laborer to haul the plastic bags of belongings away. Sometimes, seized with regret, I want to shriek, thinking of all those bits of Brendan—of us—scattered without a heart sloshing with love looking on.

Tina texts again. She and Isabel are heading to the charity shop with the remaining three bags, and then home to their families. She orders me to text her as soon as I get back from the dump *so we know ur safe*. I send a thumbs up. Seagulls wheel over the landfill, a screaming plague. The vast, tangled sea of waste comes at me in an enormous wave and fastens my breath like a stake. The place would claw at any wonder left in your head.

✑

Eamon drives me back to my parents' house, the winter dark already dropping. We arrive shortly after five o'clock, and the sight of the cleared driveway sends me into a fresh panic. I don't want to enter the empty house alone. I consider asking Eamon to drive me home instead, to the shell of what was, but I can't risk him knowing where I live. I should bolt, but I feel heavy on the passenger seat, the effort to get up and out too much. I tell Eamon about the collared doves that Dad insisted were the same two birds in his garden every day, for years.

"Plenty of stranger things are true," he says.

I reach for the door handle, rattled again. "Thanks a million."

"You're welcome. God is in the deeds, not the details."

Before I can stop myself, I crack a laugh. "Are you saying you're God?"

He smirks. "Let's leave it at God-like."

"I'm starting to think He's another delusion."

Eamon sad-smiles. "Careful. Wars have started over people saying less."

"True." I haul myself out of the car, wondering again at his crimes.

I feel him watch me as I walk away. At last he starts the engine, and I can breathe easier, but it's like my windpipe still has kinks. In my periphery, the gray BMW streaks past like a shadow.

≈

I sit in the deepening dark at Mum and Dad's kitchen table, the starless night pushing against the French doors. The rest of the world looks empty. It hits me again that soon the house will be sold. Gone. With my share of the proceeds, and those from the home I shared with Brendan, I'll press ahead with buying a new place and starting fresh. I check the back of my knee, still stinging from the dog's nails. Three thin, red scratches look back at me, so slight it seems impossible they can hurt. I half expect Eamon to reappear, and remain braced for a knock on the front door that doesn't happen.

A disturbing disappointment squats on my chest. My eyelids flutter, fighting tears. I ache to be held in strong arms, to rest my head on a broad shoulder, to nuzzle in the drift of Paco Rabanne. I check myself. I've no such notions regarding Eamon, of course, but the strange encounter loosened bolted-down feelings.

It's unnerving. Eamon's an ex-con and gangland boss who's likely a killer, and I've long hated how the media and entertainment romanticize these men. Dublin and beyond is rife with them destroying each other, along with innocent bystanders and victims of mistaken identity. What a waste—throwing themselves and others away. Thoughts of the discarded, too many gone too soon, threaten to tear me open.

Outside, the motion light is triggered, illuminating the back garden and the two ring-necked doves settling on the apple tree. I inch closer. Through the glass door, I try to study the birds' tiny heads and plump little bodies, looking for any distinctive markings. I ease open the French doors and creep outside, hoping I can get close enough before the pair fly away. I don't. I stand in the garden, watching the birds disappear into the dark. Maybe they were Dad's to believe in, and not mine. Maybe my proof of return, of the amazing that might yet remain, lies elsewhere. The clearing, emptying, I'd made plenty of space for it, hadn't I?

# THE GREAT BLUE OPEN

INSIDE GRIFFITH PARK, my five-year-old, Sorcha, pleads with me to push her higher on the swing. Maeve, older than her sister by two years, sits nearby on the riverbank, stringing daisies together. The park's two resident swans watch Maeve from a sheet of algae, as if admiring her floral necklace. The male swan is black and the female white, two faithful lovebirds my daughters long ago crowned the Queen and King of Griffith Kingdom—the sisters delighting in putting the woman first.

"Higher," Sorcha begs. I put everything I have into my next push. Right as my arms extend I am gripped by pelvic cramps, and blood spurts between my legs. Sorcha complains that I've stopped pushing her, then realizes something is wrong. She jumps from the swing, calling to her older sister.

Maeve runs toward me, her little face distorted with panic. She is a sensitive, anxious child, afraid of monsters in her pillow, bacteria eating her flesh, her and her shadow trading places, and every other torment of her imagination. My uterus contracts again, and a large, warm clot leaves me. The gelatinous blood runs down my bare legs and streaks my calves in much the same red as the king swan's beak. All I can think is that I'm emptying.

❦

The heavy bleeding persists throughout the next day. I tell myself it will soon stop, and grasp at benign explanations—early menopause or harmless fibroids—anything to defer an invasive gynie exam that never fails to humiliate, and hurt. My husband, Damien, urges me to see a doctor. I suspect he's more concerned with sex than my health. He quips that I'm not completely wrong, his laughter contagious.

The following night, inside the pub, my friends say I should demand a hysterectomy. "Have them whip it out. You don't need it anymore."

"You make me sound ancient, and with disposable parts," I say. Tipsy, my poison of choice is crisp white wine. We fall about laughing and I spill yet more menstrual blood. I don't tell them that I don't want any part of me cut away. That I don't want to be any less than I am.

Even sitting in my office, I can feel my blood drain. Not that my twelve o'clock client, Mr. Reid, could care, too busy bucking inside the chair on the other side of my desk. A couple of years back, he lent twenty-five thousand euro to his sister to open her own bakery. During the economic boom, her business thrived, but since the collapse the bakery has gone under. He wants to sue her and recover his loan.

I insist there's little he can do. He has nothing in writing regarding the debt, and his sister hasn't any assets that he can go after. Mr. Reid rants, his hot spiel punctuated every now and then with repeated slaps of his hand on my desk.

Another warm burst escapes me, adding to the heaviness of my already soaked, heavy-duty sanitary pad. I clench my pelvic muscles, trying to hold back the flow. I daren't stain my clothes or legs again in public, and most definitely not in front of Mr. Reid, still irate, still spewing. A flash of my mortified walk home from Griffith Park with Maeve and Sorcha returns in all its goriness.

"Do you hear me?" Mr. Reid says, his puffy face squashed with temper.

I wonder about his sister, if she feels crushed by this bully and her failed bakery. In my head, I encourage her to go on, to somehow go bigger. I know too many like her, including my mother. Once upon a time, Mam longed to open her own restaurant but never found the money or the luck. It didn't help that whenever she mentioned it, Dad would douse her dream: "What bank is going to lend that kind of money to a housewife, and one from Finglas to boot?"

The closest Mam ever got to restaurateur was cooking countless delicious meals for Dad and her seven children. Neighbors marveled, and even complained, saying the savory waft alone from our house roused a ferocious hunger. Eventually, whenever I mentioned the restaurant, Mam would laugh and say it was a silly idea, but I heard the catch in her voice.

Like Mam, I'd somehow let go of my burning dream. As a girl, I was obsessed with Amelia Earhart and longed to become a pilot. Nights, I'd lie on my makeshift bed on the upstairs landing, thinking how much the cratered, silvery-white moon must hate being one-of-a-kind and utterly alone. I imagined I was a second moon, and that side by side we both reigned over the vast sparkling heavens, far from the tininess of my overcrowded house, where I hadn't a real bed or a room to call my own.

"You haven't a clue," Mr. Reid says, giving my desk another wallop. "I'm off to get myself a right solicitor—someone who knows what the hell he's doing." As he leaves, I notice his labored breathing and the hang of his head. I wonder what has weighed on him over the years. I lose more fibrous blood and worry I can smell myself rotting.

⌘

On National Pet Day, Bertie's Pet Shop in town hosts a hamster derby and costume contest for the third year in a row. A first, Mam and

Dad show up to witness the antics that are now famous in our family folklore, even though our hamster, McFurry, performs dismally.

Mam curled her burgundy-dyed hair for the big event and is dressed in a powder-blue skirt suit that hugs her curves, an outfit more suited to Ladies Day at the Grand National. I watch the other women eye her, smiling to myself. She's raised the bar for the tradition, and they're furious. Dad, on the other hand, wears his signature gray wool cardigan with bulging brown buttons and black polyester trousers, the thighs smudged with gray cigarette ash. His brown, jellied eyes dart about the pet shop as if checking for all available exits. It strikes me he always has a bit of that air about him, a man trapped.

In the minutes leading up to the race, Dad feeds McFurry honey-coated treats and talks to him like he's a dog. *There's the good boy. You're going to show them, aren't you? After this, we'll be calling you Speedy!* He goes on to tell the girls he's dipped the treats in petrol, guaranteeing that a fueled-up McFurry will scamper like an Olympian and take the win. Maeve and Sorcha laugh hard. I like to watch them and Dad together. Maybe he was sometimes this funny and attentive when I was young and I just can't remember.

Dad places McFurry inside the transparent plastic ball and adds him to the crowded starting line. The girls, rocking back and forth on their feet, clap and exclaim. Right as the starting gun goes off, Dad's hand glances McFurry's neon-green ball, giving him a head start. No one else appears to notice. McFurry holds his lead for several electric seconds, then turns around inside the ball and rolls back toward the starting line. Our entire family makes frantic hand gestures and jumps up and down, shouting at McFurry to change direction. In my excitement, my uterus sheds more of its lining. I freeze, my middle clutching itself.

"Hamsters' teeth might never stop growing," Damien mutters, "but their brains sure do."

I smile, but the voice in my head won't quiet. *Cancer. Cancer. Cancer.* The previous day, I'd finally conceded the bleeding wasn't going to stop and phoned my doctor. The hospital followed up within a couple of hours and scheduled my appointment for Monday, their swift response bringing both relief and alarm.

McFurry rolls his ball and himself off the racetrack and onto the shop floor. Dad and the girls chase him down, but by the time they return, the derby is over. All is not lost. We still have the costume contest. Last year, McFurry's Ronald McDonald rigout earned him an honorable mention, and this time around the girls have high hopes of him placing in the top three, if not outright winning. Sorcha struggles to squeeze McFurry inside her doll's colorful satin dress. The hamster is transformed into a plump and pelted Snow White bursting at the seams.

"I thought he was a boy?" Dad says.

"He is," Maeve and Sorcha chorus, laughing.

Dad's face twists and the broken capillaries in his nose and cheeks rise to a purple-red. "That's not right, putting a boy in that getup."

"He's a hamster, Dad," I say.

"I know what it is," he says. This sharp version of him—this is the one who raised me.

"And no one talks like that anymore, it's homophobic," I say.

"I'm not homo anything," he says. Mam drags him off to look at turtles swimming.

The children line up with their costumed hamsters. The portly shop owner, Bertie, takes a tour of inspection, as mock-stern as an army major. Weak, headachy, I pray I won't have to stand or socialize for much longer. The pet shop doesn't have a public toilet, and I'm anxious to get home to change my pad and put my feet up.

McFurry is denied a first, second, and third place blue ribbon by, respectively, Shane MacGowan, Count Dracula, and a leprechaun.

No one could begrudge the fluffy Shane MacGowan hamster taking top place. He's decked out in a tweed cap, metal chain necklace, clip-on hoop earring, and black leather jacket with tiny red letters across its back reading *The Pogues*. Its owner, a freckled redhead, announces he wanted to glue black crepe paper to the hamster's top teeth, to match MacGowan's rotted and missing enamel, but his mam wouldn't let him. The gathering erupts in laughter.

The leprechaun is a more dubious winner, dressed only in a green felt top hat with a tiny wooden pipe taped to its chinstrap. Its owner appears next to Maeve, his long face cut with a sneer and his pipe-toting pet under his arm. "Your hamster's costume is shite."

Just as Maeve seems to have readied enough spit to fire at him, Dad steps in. He bends down, his pink hands on his knees, and pushes his florid face close to the boy's. "Why don't you go home and wash your mouth out with *shite*." He lifts Maeve into one arm and Sorcha into the other and carries them out of the pet shop on high. Mam hurries after him, warning him to mind his heart.

⤞⦵⤝

Monday afternoon, I attend my hospital appointment and undergo a uterine biopsy. Several minutes after my tissue is extracted, I still don't feel ready to stand up. Doctor Murray leaves me alone inside the examination room to recover. The pitiful gray, dimpled ceiling needs a skylight. My eyes slide to the counter, where Doctor Murray has left the pale sliver of my uterus floating inside clear solution in a jar. Above that skinless snip, tendrils of my blood perform pirouettes.

Chemicals will keep the fragment sterile until it gets to the pathologist, who will or will not declare my cells normal. I'm queasy but can't pull my eyes from the wounded slice. It's shaped like a fetus and seems to glare, outraged and accusing. It wants to get back inside me, to reattach and live.

I try to sit up a second time but, lightheaded, I flop back down. The cramping in my pelvis is so severe it's like someone is standing above my pubic bone, my middle rising and falling beneath him like a miniature trampoline.

Doctor Murray returns, her small, dull eyes at odds with her broad face and large frame. Dad would call her horsey. She hands me two white painkillers and a paper cup of cold water. "I'm sorry you feel this badly. Most women don't have this reaction." She leaves me alone again, trapped with that slimy specimen of my uterus still floating, animated, in the bloodied solution. I stare at her stethoscope, curled next to the offending jar. I slide off the exam table, struggle across the room, and secret the stethoscope into my handbag. A steal for a steal.

⤳⊗⤆

At home, Damien asks again why Doctor Murray would perform a biopsy. He says *biopsy* like the word is so huge he can barely hold it in his mouth. He goes on about the biopsy as he paces round the kitchen table. "They can't think...they don't think...do they?" There's something behind his alarm, a note of near excitement that suggests he's almost gladdened by the possibility of crisis, a break from the ordinary.

I laugh lightly. "When I'm gone, you'll have another woman in here in no time."

"Don't say that," he says. "How could you say that?"

I suddenly know it's true. He's no swan. His theatrics and the gripping, cinching pain in my pelvis force me upstairs.

In bed, I cling to the rubber hot water bottle, holding it to my middle with both arms. The entire area below my navel feels laced with acid. At last the painkiller kicks in and I start to drift. I'm almost asleep when Maeve and Sorcha climb onto my bed, their full lips turned down and their foreheads creased.

"Daddy said you're sick," Sorcha says.

"You're not going to die, are you?" Maeve asks.

"You," I say, smiling. "Little Miss Worry."

I remember Doctor Murray's stethoscope and send them back downstairs. They return, their mood lifted by the surprise medical instrument. We listen to each other's hearts. Next, we listen to our own hearts. Maeve and Sorcha marvel at how they'd never before heard a heartbeat—not like this, so clear and loud and strong. The only other time I have heard a heartbeat with such clarity was when I was pregnant with each of them. The girls continue to listen to their own hearts, showing off tiny teeth and pink fleshy gums. I can't stop seeing the sliver of my uterus inside Doctor Murray's office, like a shred of boiled ham.

If the hospital phones tomorrow, it won't be good. I've heard enough horror stories to know that results that soon can mean only one thing. I imagine the call comes early in the afternoon and that the phone doesn't ring, but drills. When I answer, I grip the receiver and hold my breath. Those first few seconds, I allow myself to believe Doctor Murray only wants to ask if I have any idea where her stethoscope could have gotten to. Then she speaks, and tells me the worst.

The girls and I keep passing around the stethoscope, our eyes shiny. It's like we can't stop. Like nothing else has ever brought such wonder.

"Tell me about your dreams?" I ask.

"I have bad dreams," Maeve begins.

"Not like that," I say gently. "What do you both want to be when you grow up?"

They rush to tell me—actor, ballerina, ice cream server, singer, fashion designer, makeup artist.

"Don't ever stop dreaming," I say. "Don't ever stop believing that dreams can come true. Promise me."

⚘

The next morning drags. I try to work but can't concentrate, worry and painkillers clouding my mind. At least my pelvis no longer feels like it's on fire, but my blood loss remains steady. The minutes wind past, and still Doctor Murray doesn't phone. I tell myself that's good news. By noon, Damien has already called, wanting to know if I've heard anything. He insists I contact Doctor Murray's office. I do, but my results aren't ready.

I've no meetings on today's calendar and I won't be needed in court until tomorrow. I make a call regarding a property title dispute, but the auctioneer involved isn't available. I don't phone my friends or my mother. The only person I've told about the biopsy is Damien. I imagine this somehow makes me brave and heroic. I try online shopping, but can't stop myself from consulting Doctor Google and self-diagnosing my impending demise. Outside, a plane flies low over our office building. Long after the aircraft passes, it's still roaring in my head.

I take my lunch break and drive to the airport. I park on the Old Airport Road to the rear of the terminals and watch the planes land and takeoff. When I was a girl, Dad sometimes took Mam and my six brothers and me here. Weather permitting, we'd sit on top of our car and track the planes. During bad weather—rain, gales, frost—we'd stay inside the car and repeatedly wipe the condensation from the windows. We made up stories about the passengers overhead, imagining where they were going to and coming from.

I reserved my best stories for the pilots, all women, all superheroes. One woman captain was transporting her passengers to an alternate dimension in a desperate bid to reinvent and improve the human race. The portal to this mirror world and second chance lay inside a certain cloud that needed to be entered at a certain time, and angle, and speed. Another woman captain was carrying the greatest minds in the world to a secret island, where they would solve every ill known to humankind and in that way save us all. I never told anyone these stories. They would dismiss them, just like they dismissed me. People said I'd never be a pilot. Said I needed to grow up. I don't remember when I started to believe them.

⟊⟐⟐

I don't return to work, but call in sick. I drive out of the city to the National Flight Centre, the radio on full blast so I can't hear my nerves and doubts.

I push myself toward the Flight Centre's reception desk, hoping the platinum-haired receptionist can't tell I'm shaking. I inquire about lessons and getting my pilot's license, so emotional I don't recognize my own voice. To my surprise, and fright, she tells me visibility and weather conditions are good and that I can take my first in-flight lesson here and now. It hurts to peel my tongue from the roof of my parched mouth.

"Wait. I get to fly today? But this will be my first lesson ever. I haven't a clue what I'm doing."

She reassures me, amused, that I'll be vetted and prepped, and all going well I will shortly be airborne. "So brace yourself."

I falter yet again as she talks me through the total costs, the amount of study, and the number of flights it will actually take to obtain my pilot's license, a level of commitment I can barely grasp. I agree to this single lesson and training flight. "Are you sure? It's much cheaper to go with a package deal."

"I'm sure." I surrender my credit card, fighting a mounting panic.
I take a seat in the white, clinical reception area and complete
the necessary paperwork. Several times I almost leave, but this might
be my one and only chance. My swan song. It seems impossible that
they're allowing me to fly today with no prior study or training. I
leaf through a glossy magazine, trying to calm myself. Pale, vacant
supermodels stare up from the magazine's smooth pages. They look
like sculptures with too much carved away, little between their vital
organs and the outside world but skin and skeleton. I return the magazine to the side table and pull my jacket tighter, wrapping myself.

At last, my instructor appears. He looks to be in his mid-fifties
and wears a brown leather pilot jacket, distressed jeans, and scuffed
green combat boots. His gray-brown ponytail sits on his back like
frayed rope. Tom's accent is English. "Macclesfield," he says. As we
walk, he tells me that he likes fast machines—planes, boats, cars.
"The Triumph," he says, "now that's top of its class."

❦

Inside the simulated cockpit, Tom delivers an overview of flight dy-
namics and acquaints me with the plane's various dials and controls.
He quizzes me afterward and I duly point to the yoke, pitch, yaw,
and more.

"You're a natural," he says, grinning. He asks me why I want to fly.

I try to laugh off the question. "I think I was a bird in a former life."

"And now you're on your way to becoming a pilot in this one,
lovely."

"We'll see about that." I struggle to keep my smile.

If only I'd started flight lessons twenty years ago, when I was
fresh from school. I became a solicitor because I wanted to make
things more equal and right in the world, and to show people I *could*

be someone. Only I wasn't the someone I most wanted to be. Now it might be too late. I think of my mother and her restaurant that never was. I'm doing this for her, too, and for Mr. Reid's sister who lost her bakery. For everyone with dead dreams.

Tom escorts me out to the waiting plane. I still can't quite believe this is happening. To my further amazement, Tom tells me I can fly wherever I want. "Within reason," he adds, laughing. "We only have forty minutes and so much fuel."

We don bulky headphones, and Tom powers on the plane's engine. The tinny craft shakes like an old battered elevator. He has full control of the takeoff, but promises that once we're in the air, amid the clouds, I'll at long last become the pilot. He grins and raises a vigorous thumbs up. I imagine he and I kissing. It's not so much that I'm attracted to him but that I want to build on this mad risk I've taken. I'm so exhilarated I almost can't bear it, my throat full, head dizzy, and veins fizzing.

When I finally take command of the plane, there's a terrific rush of terror, and then it's as if I'm released from myself and cast adrift in an out-of-body experience. I'm not flying through the sky—I am the sky, and have never felt this expansive or ecstatic. I soar over my old street and right above the redbrick house where I grew up. I picture my parents below, Mam peeling potatoes at the kitchen sink and Dad sitting in his armchair in the corner, soaking his bunioned feet in a basin of steaming, salted water. I want to shout. "Look up! Look at me!"

I fly over my empty golden-yellow house, the girls at school, Damien at work. I imagine the three of them standing in our front garden, in the center of our small rectangle of grass. They look up, waving and cheering. I'm grinning so hard my cheeks hurt. I have never felt this bold, or free. I push away the thought that this is what it would be like in the next life: me looking down at my husband and daughters, at everyone and everything I've left behind.

The next morning, I again phone Doctor Murray's office, the sickening, churning sensations in my stomach at an all-time high. I'm told in solemn tones that the doctor is with a patient, but my results are available and can be delivered by a nurse. I'm transferred, my hand sweating on the phone receiver. The nurse delivers my biopsy results deadpan, her nasal accent ringing of the depths of the west coast. She's the older nurse, I believe, with the white streaks in her hair like swirls of cream in coffee.

"Negative," she repeats. She schedules me for a follow-up appointment, to insert an IUD contraceptive with hormones that will thin out the lining of my uterus. "That should right you."

I lie in bed next to Damien while he sleeps, my negative result still a secret. I will tell him in the morning, first thing. I couldn't bring myself to say anything earlier, knowing we will both feel strangely bereft once the news is shared and the sense of urgency dissipated. I didn't tell him or anyone else about my flying lesson, either, afraid that elation would be similarly diminished.

Years ago, I told Damien I was an Amelia Earhart fanatic, and about the tall tales I'd made up as a girl of superhero women pilots. I shared my own desire to commandeer the skies. "You were a kid," he said. "Sure we all thought up stupid stuff back then." He attempted to nuzzle my neck and reach for my breast. I never did tell him it was the worst thing he could have said and done—something else for me to reveal tomorrow.

Doctor Murray's stethoscope on my nightstand tugs. I place its buds in my ears, hold the cold chest piece to my heart, and listen to its four chambers drum in the night, faster, louder, about to take off. I climb the skies and fly over the city, reveling in my God's-eye view. I hover above rows of houses with dark roofs, acres of lush green, and somewhere inside the glittering river, the Queen and King of Griffith Kingdom, the swans parting the water while I slice open the sky.

# ACKNOWLEDGMENTS

My DEEP THANKS to Michelle Dotter, Dan Wickett, and the entire Dzanc Books team for selecting *In the Event of Contact* for the 2019 Short Story Collection Prize. I remain delighted and honored. Michelle Dotter is an excellent, tireless editor and publisher who brought out the best in this collection, and in me. Matt Revert, thank you for my book cover; the loveliest skin for these stories.

Thanks to the editors who first published work from this collection, and to the readers and writers who've guided and encouraged me over the long, twisty way—notably my wonderful community at the Writers Grotto. I'm an ardent fan of the authors who provided praise for this book and am thrilled each took the time and care to read and cheer for these stories.

I am forever grateful to my family and friends for their unfailing support and patience, especially my two daughters. Finally, thank you to the girl and young adult I was—crushed but still standing.

Photo by Justin Yee

# ABOUT THE AUTHOR

ETHEL ROHAN won the 2019 Dzanc Short Story Collection Prize with her new collection, *In the Event of Contact*. Her debut novel *The Weight of Him* (St. Martin's Press and Atlantic Books, 2017) was an Amazon, *Bustle*, KOBO, and *San Francisco Chronicle* Best Book. *The Weight of Him* won a Plumeri Fellowship, Silver Nautilus Award, the Northern California Publishers and Authors' Award, and was shortlisted for the Reading Women Award.

She is also the author of two story collections, *Goodnight Nobody* and *Cut Through the Bone*, the former longlisted for The Edge Hill Prize and the latter longlisted for The Story Prize. She was longlisted for *The Sunday Times* EFG Short Story Award, winner of the Bryan MacMahon Short Story Award, and shortlisted for the CUIRT, Roberts, and Bristol Short Story Prizes.

Her work has appeared in *The New York Times, World Literature Today, PEN America, The Washington Post, Tin House, The Irish Times*, and *GUERNICA*, among many others. She has reviewed books for *New York Journal of Books* and elsewhere.

Born and raised in Dublin, Ireland, Rohan lives in San Francisco where she received her MFA in fiction from Mills College and is a member of The Writers Grotto.